wε

CONFESSION!

Mayhem ripped through Red Rock, Texas, late yesterday when Clint Lockhart revealed a sinister secret. The Double Crown ranch hand and brother-in-law to Ryan Fortune confessed to murdering Sophia Fortune and framing Lily Cassidy, fiancée to Ryan, for the hideous crime.

Lockhart delivered another earth-shattering revelation: he and Sophia, estranged wife of Ryan, had masterminded the kidnapping of Bryan Fortune in an evil get-rich-quick scheme. But their hired thugs stole the wrong baby—the child now cared for by Matthew and Claudia Fortune, little toddling Taylor. Tragically, baby Bryan's disappearance and whereabouts remain a mystery. Looks as if the locked-up Lockhart is in for a dose of justice—Texas style....

An exuberant Lily Cassidy was cleared of all charges soon after Lockhart's guilt was disclosed. She and Ryan are planning a rush marriage—nothing like shedding prison stripes for white satin!

Even in the midst of tragedy and media chaos...romance sparks. Every-girl's-dream-man Zane Fortune has plucked Gwen Hutton, struggling single mom, from obscurity—and is parading her around town as his fiancée! Is this setup too quick-'n'-easy to be the real deal...or are Zane's true feelings as nuclear as those oh-so-public kisses...?

About the Author

JACKIE MERRITT

is still writing, just not with the speed and constancy of
years past. She and her husband are living in southern
Nevada again, falling back on old habits of loving the
long, warm or slightly cool winters and trying almost
desperately to head north for the months of July and
August, when the fiery sun bakes people and cacti alike.

JACKIE MERRITT
Hired Bride

Published by Silhouette Books
America's Publisher of Contemporary Romance

Special thanks and acknowledgment are given
to Jackie Merritt for her contribution
to THE FORTUNES OF TEXAS series.

 SILHOUETTE BOOKS

ISBN 0-373-38925-6

HIRED BRIDE

Copyright © 1999 by Harlequin Books S.A.

This edition published by arrangement with Harlequin Books S.A.

® and TM are trademarks of Harlequin Books S.A., used under license. Trademarks indicated with ® are registered in the United States Patent and Trademark Office, the Canadian Trade Marks Office and in other countries.

Visit Silhouette Books at www.eHarlequin.com

Printed in U.S.A.

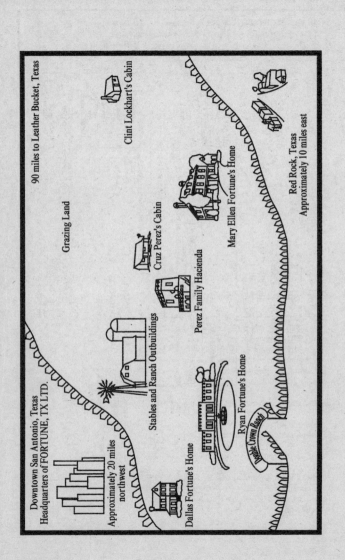

THE FORTUNES OF TEXAS

KINGSTON FORTUNE (d)

1st marriage
PATIENCE TALBOT (d)
Teddy§

2nd marriage
SELENA HOBBS (d)

- - - CAMERON (d)
m MARY ELLEN LOCKHART

RYAN
1st marriage
JANINE LOCKHART (d)

MIRANDA
m Lloyd Carter (D)

KANE GABRIELLE ⑧
m
Wyatt
Grayhawk

MATTHEW ZANE ⑫   VANESSA ② ***VICTORIA ⑩
m   m
Claudia Beaumont   Devin Kincaid   Quinn McCoy
Bryan

DALLAS ④
1st marriage m
Sara Andersen (d)
2nd marriage m
Maggie Perez

† ROSITA and RUBEN PEREZ

Anita Carmen Frieda CRUZ ③
                                          m
                                    Savannah
                                    Clark

MAGGIE ④
1st marriage
m
Craig Randall (D)
2nd marriage
m
Travis
Dallas Fortune

2nd marriage
SOPHIA BARNES

- - - CLINT LOCKHART
brother of
JACE LOCKHART ⑥
m
Ciara Wilde

HOLDEN ① LOGAN ⑨ EDEN ⑦
m   m
Lucinda   Amanda Sheikh
Brightwater Sue*   Ben
                        Ramir

LILY
REDGROVE

m Emily
Applegate

James a.k.a.
Taylor

Sawyer*

COLE* ⑪ HANNAH ⑤ MARIA
m   m
Annie   Parker
Jones   Malone

Chester Cassidy (d)

TITLES:

1. MILLION DOLLAR MARRIAGE
2. THE BABY PURSUIT
3. EXPECTING...IN TEXAS
4. A WILLING WIFE
5. A MAN OF HONOR
6. SNOWBOUND CINDERELLA
7. THE SHEIKH'S SECRET SON
8. THE HEIRESS AND THE SHERIFF
9. LONE STAR WEDDING
10. IN THE ARMS OF A HERO
11. WED BY A WEDDING?!
12. HIRED BRIDE

* Child of affair
d Deceased
D Divorced
m Married
*** Twins
† Affair
§ Loyal ranch staff
§ Kidnapped by maternal grandfather

THE F☘RTUNES OF TEXAS™

🏵 *Meet the Fortunes of Texas* 🏵

Zane Fortune: The marriage-shy executive needed a pretend fiancée to outsmart his family's matchmaking plans. Would Zane's scheme backfire and have him setting his sights on his hired bride becoming his real-life wife?

Gwen Hutton: The single mother had her hands full raising her three young children—she didn't need her charming rogue boss reminding her how it felt to be a woman...or did she?

Baby Bryan: His whereabouts have been a mystery for months. And law enforcement officials are hoping that some new leads they've uncovered will help them crack the case of the century.

Ryan Fortune: The patriarch has steadfastly held the family together during their time of turmoil. Dare he hope that he will be reunited with his grandson and that he will soon marry his lady love Lily?

One

"Zane, I'm so sorry to leave you hanging like this, but I have to fly to Fort Worth this weekend. My sister Glenda just phoned, and our mother is in the hospital again. Apparently she's had another heart attack. Glenda said Mother's doctors told her that the attack was rather mild, but Mother is frightened and wants her children around her. I know I promised to attend Mr. Malone's wedding with you this weekend, but as things stand now I have to back out. I hope you understand."

Zane Fortune was seated behind his massive mahogany desk, and given his secretary's plaintive expression and his own compassion for anyone in danger of losing a parent, he had no choice but to say, "Heather, of course I understand. Don't give it another thought. In fact, leave today." It was Friday afternoon, and he certainly could manage without Heather for one afternoon, even if she was his right arm at the office.

Zane was executive director of marketing at Fortune TX, Ltd. It was a title of no small importance as the corporation's ventures were so diversified—real estate development, plastics, computer manufacturing, to name a few—that marketing was a high-priority department. Zane headed a team of marketing experts that were the best to be had, and not just in Texas, either.

Heather was a calming influence for Zane when things got hectic in his department. She was a top-notch secretary who could juggle a dozen important jobs at the same time without becoming unhinged, or even ruffled. Zane felt very fortunate to have Heather Moore for his private secretary, and he would do just about anything to keep her happy with her job. ''Really, Heather, I mean it. Leave right away. And please take all the time you need.''

''Thank you, Zane. I was hoping you'd say that,'' Heather murmured. ''I checked your calendar, and the rest of your day is relatively free.'' She laid the papers she'd been holding on Zane's desk. ''If you'll sign these letters, I'll put them in the mail before I leave.''

Zane scanned the letters he'd dictated that morning and scrawled his name on each of them. He handed them back with a kindly, ''I sincerely hope your mother recovers, Heather.'' Zane's own mother had died when he was sixteen, and every so often that awful, empty sense of loss would still sneak up on him.

''Thank you. From what Glenda told me, I'm sure she will.'' Heather took the letters and added quietly, ''This time.'' She brightened her countenance. ''I'll see you on Monday, Zane. I left a list of Fort Worth phone numbers on my desk, just in case you should need to talk to me during the weekend.''

''Thanks, Heather.'' Watching his secretary hurry out, Zane sat back in his chair and frowned. He'd been counting on Heather's company during the upcoming weekend to throw his matchmaking sisters and sisters-in-law a curve. For some reason the women in his vast family had decided it was time he settled down, and lately they had started parading their single female friends in front of him with what Zane believed was a hope that he would be struck dumb by Cupid's arrow.

It wasn't Zane's nature to tell them with unequivocal conviction to lay off so he'd come up with the idea of attending the most current get-together—the wedding of his friends Parker Malone and Hannah Cassidy—with an attractive woman on his arm. The members of his family knew that Heather was his secretary, of course, but he had explained his predicament to Heather and she had agreed to put on a little show for any of the Fortunes who might be interested in Zane's love life, to act as though their relationship had gone beyond what it really was. As attractive as Heather was, she'd had a steady boyfriend for a long time, and her relationship with Zane was strictly business.

Now he'd have to go to Parker's wedding alone, Zane thought with a put-upon sigh. He'd come up with Heather as his date because she wouldn't have read anything into his plan that he hadn't intended, whereas the ladies in his little black book might get all sorts of ideas from a weekend affair with the Fortunes. Why couldn't the females in his family just leave him be? So what if he was the only unmarried child of Ryan Fortune, the last holdout? His brothers Matthew and Dallas were married, as were his sisters Victoria and Vanessa. But was his bachelor status anyone's business but his own?

Memories suddenly assailed Zane, and his frown deepened. He had almost reached the altar himself one time, with a beautiful young woman, Melanie Wilson.

Melanie had changed her mind at the last minute—
declaring with a pretty pout that she just wasn't ready
to settle down—and, ever since, Zane had been very
cautious with his feelings. He liked women, he enjoyed their company, but he rarely dated the same
woman more than a few times.

Women liked him. Zane knew that he'd broken
more than one female heart in and around San Antonio, but the second that he felt a woman was looking
for more than friendship or an *affaire d'amour,* he
dropped her. He wasn't particularly proud of his track
record, but he simply could not bring himself to behave any other way. Commitment was a serious step;
he'd taken it once and gotten badly burned. It was an
experience he didn't wish to repeat.

Pulling himself out of the past, Zane made a few
business calls, then decided to quit for the day. He
rarely left the office early, but it had been a rough
week, so today he'd go home, change into comfortable
clothes and while away the rest of the day in quiet
relaxation. It would be a pleasant change of pace. He
might even be able to stop resenting his matchmaking
family for a few hours. The weekend wedding cele-
bration was, after all, scheduled to begin tomorrow,
and now he wasn't looking forward to it at all. Damn
shame too, because he *had* been, until Heather backed
out.

After making one more phone call to let David Hancock—the person who acted as marketing director
when Zane was out of the office—know that he was
leaving for the day, Zane took his briefcase and de-
parted.

During the elevator ride to the first floor, Zane
checked his watch. It was only a little after two, and

he couldn't remember the last time he'd left that early without a darn good reason. Today he had no reason at all, merely a disquietude in his gut. He actually thought of faking illness—a bout with the flu would be enough—and calling Parker to tell his friend that even if he happened to feel a little better in the morning, he shouldn't be spreading germs at the wedding. Parker would be disappointed, of course, but Zane could almost hear him saying, "Hell, man, stay in bed and get well. If you can't make it, you can't make it."

In the parking garage, Zane loosened his tie and walked to his car. During the drive to Kingston Estates, the upscale community where his large, beautiful home was located, he changed his mind fifty times. One minute, he knew that he had to attend the wedding; the next, he knew that he'd have such a miserable time avoiding all the traps set by his sisters and sisters-in-law that he could hardly bear thinking about the weekend.

Zane loved his big family, but sometimes they drove him up the wall. One or more of them also worried the hell out of him at times, but other than the unsolved kidnapping of his nephew Bryan, the child of Matthew and Claudia, Zane's brother and sister-in-law, things had pretty much settled down in the family. It sure had been a mess for a while, though, what with his father's fiancée, Lily Cassidy, having been charged with the murder of Ryan's second wife, Sophia, whom he'd been trying to divorce, so he could marry Lily. Zane couldn't believe they'd discovered the real murderer was his uncle—Clint Lockhart. But with Clint in custody, Lily had been exonerated, and even while her daughter Hannah had been planning her own wedding to Parker, she had been working on preparations for Ryan and Lily's wedding as well. From what Zane had heard thus far, it was going to be a very special occasion.

So Hannah was going to be Zane's stepsister, which made her and Parker's upcoming wedding no trivial event. Zane knew he should be there, in spite of the personal misgivings that cast a dark shadow on the affair. He was only twenty-nine years old, for crying out loud, certainly not so old that Claudia and his sisters should take up a crusade to get him married. The whole thing just rubbed him wrong, no matter how he looked at it.

Disgruntled and out of sorts because he couldn't seem to reach a decision he felt he could live with, Zane finally pulled into the wide circular driveway of his home and parked at the front door. Fat lot of relaxing he'd be doing with this problem on his mind he thought cynically as he got out of the car.

Taking his mail from the mailbox, he unlocked his front door and stepped into the elegant foyer. Zane's Australian shepherd, Alamo, always greeted him at the door, no matter what time of day or night he came home. But today he wasn't there. Then Zane heard Alamo barking and running through the house, toenails clicking on tile, obviously a little late today, but on his way, nevertheless.

Alamo suddenly rounded a corner and, barking happily and loudly, took a flying leap at his master. Zane recoiled, because the dog was dripping water and soapsuds, and now *he* was wet and soapy, as well. Or rather, his expensive tailor-made suit was.

He had only a second to think about it before a young woman skidded and slid around the same corner, shouting, "Alamo! Darn it, what's wrong with you today?'' At the sight of Zane standing there, her eyes got big and she ground to a halt, mumbling, ''Uh, you're Zane Fortune.''

Zane wasn't exactly polite. ''If you count Alamo, that makes three of us who know who I am. What I'd like to know is who are you, and what in hell is going on in here?'' he growled. However unnerving this little scenario was, Zane couldn't help admiring the figure defined behind the sopping wet T-shirt and old jeans. Whoever she was, she had a drop-dead body. Her face, even crimson with embarrassment, was startlingly pretty, and her long, sun-streaked light brown hair, though flying every which way, was fabulous.

The lady obviously got her wits together because she lifted her chin almost defiantly and said, ''I'm Gwen Hutton. I was bathing Alamo, and he must have heard you come in because he suddenly jumped out of the tub. I tried to hold him back, which is why I'm so soggy, but he got away from me, and now you're all wet too. I hope your suit isn't ruined.''

Alamo tried to climb Zane's legs, and Zane issued a quiet command. ''Down, boy.'' The dog instantly obeyed and lay with his nose on his front paws.

''Let me get this straight,'' Zane said. ''You're the person who's been bathing my dog for the past several months?''

''Among other things, yes,'' Gwen replied evenly. ''Your secretary, Heather Moore, employed my company, Help-Mate, to do some of the things you apparently don't have time to do yourself.''

''Never even heard of a company called Help-Mate.''

''Yes, well, as I said, I've been dealing with your secretary.'' Gwen was catching on to Zane Fortune's interest in her wet T-shirt. Maybe more unsettling than that, though, was finally standing face-to-face with a man she'd known only through photographs, which wouldn't amount to a hill of beans if she hadn't thought him to be the best-looking guy she'd ever seen.

Actually, the photos she'd run across in his house and in the society pages of the newspaper didn't do him justice. He really was too handsome to be believed, with his perfect features, dark blond hair and electric-blue eyes. And he was taller than she'd expected, at least six feet tall, with broad shoulders and an athletically lean build.

Small wonder he had such a fast reputation, Gwen thought with an inner sigh. Any man who looked like this probably had to beat women off with a stick.

"And you have a key to my house?" Zane asked.

"I'm licensed and bonded, Mr. Fortune, and there is no way I could do what I do without having access to a client's home." Gwen plucked the wet fabric of her T-shirt away from her chest, hoping it wouldn't immediately adhere to her body again. Zane Fortune couldn't seem to keep his eyes off her bosom, and she knew that her nipples were showing right through her bra and T-shirt.

"Uh, what else do you do besides bathe dogs?" Zane was getting a glimmer of an idea, but he needed to know more about Gwen Hutton before advancing it.

"For you, or for clients in general?"

"For clients in general."

"Mr. Fortune, I'm very willing to discuss my company with you, but don't you think you should get a towel or something and at least try to save your suit?"

"Forget the suit. Tell me about your company. And let's get out of the foyer. I'd like something cold to drink, so let's continue this discussion in the kitchen."

"I really should finish bathing Alamo."

"Makes sense. Tell you what. I'll go and change clothes, and you finish up with Alamo. Then we'll meet in the kitchen and have a cold drink together."

Gwen took a look at her waterproof watch. "I have another appointment in about thirty minutes, so I don't have a lot of time to spare."

Zane grinned, and Gwen's heart actually skipped a beat at the sight of his incredible smile and snowy white teeth.

She instantly chided herself for such a foolish reaction to a simple smile. *What the heck is wrong with you? He's a client, and even if he wasn't, he is not your kind of man. He's filthy rich and probably spoiled rotten, and he is exactly the sort of man that a decent, hardworking woman should stay completely away from.*

"I'm sure you can squeeze a ten-minute conversation into your busy schedule," Zane said as he started away. "Meet you in the kitchen."

"Come on, Alamo," Gwen said with a frown caused by what had sounded like amusement in Fortune's comment. If he thought her dedication to duty was funny, then there was no way she could even let herself like him as a person. She was a widow with three small children to support, definitely not a laughing matter. In fact, she would bet anything that she put in more hours a day to earn a living than Zane Fortune did.

Of course, he didn't *need* to earn a living. Everyone in this part of Texas knew that the Fortunes had been

wealthy for generations. Actually, Gwen had to give
Zane points for working at all, when he could simply
slide through life on old money, should he choose.
Still, she and everybody else knew that executives in
large companies had it pretty cushy, what with golf
and tennis games during working hours, two-hour
lunch breaks and secretaries up the kazoo to do the
real work.

Well, that was none of her business she told herself
while urging Alamo back into the tub so she could
rinse away the soapsuds clinging to his coat. She
worked fast, and when the suds were gone she turned
the dog into the massive indoor pool room so he could
shake away the water to his heart's content without
spreading it all over the house.

When Gwen first started her business, she'd been in
awe of some of the homes belonging to wealthy clients. For instance, Zane Fortune's home had two
swimming pools, one outside and one inside. It had a
tennis court and a putting green, and the grounds were
lavishly landscaped. The house itself was a dream,
contemporary in style, very large and professionally
decorated.

Now, after almost a year of visiting luxury homes
to do various chores, Gwen still admired but was no
longer awestruck. She would never rub elbows with
San Antonio's rich and famous, and it didn't bother
her a bit. Her entire life was focused on her kids, on
earning enough money to give them the necessities in
the present and on trying very hard to save some for
their future. It seemed, however, that whenever she
accumulated any amount of cash, something came up
that forced her to spend it. Gwen often worried about

how she would pay for a college education for each of her children.

With handfuls of paper towel, she hurriedly wiped up the puddles left by Alamo during his race to the front door. She also used paper towels on herself, sopping up some of the water from her clothes. Untying the ribbon that held her hair back from her face—or was supposed to—she finger-combed straying strands back into place and retied the ribbon. She had just finished doing what she could to make herself more presentable when Zane returned to the kitchen. He was wearing baggy gray sweatpants, a mismatched blue top and old tennis shoes without socks.

His apparel surprised Gwen. Now he looked very much as she did. No, that wasn't true. He was still so handsome that she found it difficult to look directly at him. It was a discomfiting feeling, one she didn't much care for. Men didn't daunt her, for Pete's sake. Not normally, they didn't.

"Oh, good, you're still here," Zane said, and he opened the refrigerator door. "So, what would you like to drink?"

"Nothing, Mr. Fortune, but thank you. I really don't have the time to—"

"I'm only asking for a few minutes, Gwen. And for heaven's sake, darlin', call me Zane. Now, how about an orange juice? Or a soda?"

That *darlin'* had rolled off his tongue so smoothly that it never occurred to Gwen that Zane might mean something by it. And obviously, he wasn't going to let her leave without his "ten-minute" discussion, though she couldn't imagine what he wanted to talk to her about. Unless there was something else he would like her to be doing for him as Help-Mate. He was a client, after all.

"All right," she said, giving in gracefully, though she should already have left this house and been on her way to her next appointment. "I'll have a bottle of water, if you have it."

"Sure do." Zane took their drinks from the refrigerator and let the door swing shut. "Let's sit down." He carried her water and his orange juice to the table. "Would you like a glass?"

"The bottle is fine, thanks." Gwen took the chair that was directly across the table from the one Zane chose. He loosened the bottle cap and handed her the water.

Immediately she was uncomfortable under his intense scrutiny. He seemed to be trying to see beneath her skin. What was he hoping to do, read her mind? She certainly had no secrets. This whole meeting struck her as strange.

"Tell me what you do for your company," Zane said.

Gwen frowned. "I'm not sure I understand what you'd like to know."

"I'd like to know the scope of your duties. Besides bathing dogs, what else do you do?"

"Aren't you aware of the other things I do for you?"

Zane sat back, thought a moment, then looked slightly startled. "I think I'm beginning to get the picture. Besides bathing Alamo, you're the person who's been cleaning my house, tending to my laundry and dry cleaning, buying my groceries, et cetera, et cetera."

"Yes, there are a number of etceteras," Gwen said

dryly. "With most of my clients, to be honest. Help-Mate was designed to assist busy people with chores they have no time to do themselves. Things a wife or husband might do if the client had a spouse with extra time."

"Are all of your clients unmarried?" Zane asked, and took a swallow of his orange juice while looking into Gwen Hutton's lovely blue-gray eyes.

Her gaze didn't waver, though she did wonder why he kept looking at her so intently. "A few of them are married, or living with someone, but most are single."

"Like me." Zane took a breath, and Gwen sensed it was a preamble to something—probably his reason for delaying her departure. "Gwen," he said, "I have a problem, and I think you just might be the answer."

She became wary, concerned about the personal note she heard in his voice, but she said slowly, "I'm listening."

"I'm going to ask you something, and I hope you won't be offended, but have you ever done any escorting?"

Her eyes widened, and she started to get up from her chair. "Mr. Fortune, if I've given you any reason to think—"

Holding up a hand, Zane broke in. "I'm not suggesting anything immoral or illegal. Please don't rush into an erroneous opinion before you give me a chance to explain my question."

Gwen slowly sank back to the chair. "All right," she said flatly. "Explain." *And make it good, because if you don't I'll be crossing you off my client list!* It wasn't a pleasant thought. She needed every client she had worked so hard to obtain. Spent money to obtain, as a matter of fact. Advertising was costly, and she was always grateful when a potential new customer mentioned phoning Help-Mate because he or she had seen one of her little ads.

"What I'm going to propose to you is a simple business arrangement. I need an attractive lady to escort to a wedding this weekend. I realize there are women for hire out there, but I wouldn't insult my family and friends in that manner. Here's the situation. The females in my family have decided that I should be married, or at least committed to one woman. They have taken it upon themselves to find me a wife, and I know that there'll be at least a dozen unmarried women at that wedding just waiting to pounce on me."

"Why don't you just tell the females in your family to leave you alone?" Gwen asked, suspicion and distrust in every syllable. She had never heard a more lame story in her life. If that was Zane Fortune's favorite line, it was a wonder he got anywhere with decent women. The thing was, she enjoyed reading the society section of the newspaper and knew that Zane *did* attract decent women. So what, really, was this all about?

Zane heaved a sigh. "I wish I could do that. Actually, I've tried to do that, but it never comes off the way I'd like it to. My sisters think I'm kidding around with them, they kid back and the whole thing falls apart.

"Anyway, I came up with an idea to at least get me through the weekend relatively unscathed. Heather, my secretary, was going to attend the wedding with me, and we were going to lead everyone to believe that she and I had become an item. It's not true, of course. Heather's practically engaged. But she agreed to help me out, and then today she received a phone call from her sister in Fort Worth. Their mother is in the hospital, and naturally Heather had to go and see her.''

"And you…you'd like me to take her place?'' Gwen was still guarded, but she was beginning to believe that Zane wasn't handing her a line.

"Exactly. I'm not asking you to give up your weekend for nothing, Gwen. I'll pay you a thousand dollars if you go to that wedding with me and act as though we are *very* good friends.''

She managed not to gasp, but she couldn't prevent a weakly parroted, "A thousand dollars?''

"Make it two thousand," Zane said quickly, reading her reaction as reluctance. "This is important to me, Gwen, and I'm willing to pay for two days of your time. Is two thousand enough?''

"Uh…yes. Two thousand is, uh, sufficient.'' Was accepting money for spending time with a man immoral, even though she would be committing no definitively immoral acts? Goodness knows, she could use the money. She lived from day to day, working herself into an early grave to make ends meet, always with that nagging worry about her children's future. With a windfall of two thousand dollars…well, there was so much she could do with it, she really wouldn't know where to start.

But just what did Zane Fortune expect for so much money?

She said what she'd been thinking, keeping her voice at an even pitch though her pulse was racing. "Before I give you an answer, Mr. Fortune, tell me exactly what you expect for your money.''

Two

Ramona Garcia was two things to Gwen—a reliable, loving baby-sitter and a good friend. The baby-sitting had come first, and the friendship had developed because Ramona and Gwen had so much in common. Very close in age, they were both widows with small children—Ramona had two little ones and Gwen had three. In one way, however, Ramona was more fortunate than Gwen. Ramona's husband had left her a sizable insurance policy, which, while it didn't make her a wealthy woman, certainly made her life easier than Gwen's. Ramona had invested the insurance money in an annuity with monthly draws, and she supplemented that income with childcare in her own home. When Gwen became a steady customer, Ramona stopped taking in other children. At that point her income had become satisfactory.

Gwen had often asked herself why she had permitted her husband Paul to procrastinate on buying life insurance, but in her heart she knew the answer to that question as well as she knew anything: Paul simply had not been a worrier or a planner. Like many people with happy-go-lucky personalities, Paul had enjoyed today and rarely thought of tomorrow.

At any rate, Gwen had been left with a mortgaged house, two cars and a boat with monthly payments, and no income beyond a modest monthly social security check. If her parents hadn't helped her out financially after Paul's fatal accident, Gwen would have lost the little she did have. Her father had stepped in and sold the boat and one of the cars, eliminating two of her debts, and he had made the payments on her mortgage and the other car for two months. By then Gwen had pulled herself together and faced her situation; she could not live off her folks indefinitely. It was time she shaped up and started supporting herself.

Her biggest hurdle to finding a job that paid enough to support herself was her lack of training. Before meeting Paul, she had been in college to become an art teacher, and though she was talented in many art forms, there weren't a lot of jobs for wannabe artists out there. She had wished many times that she had the abilities to work as a secretary, but wishes didn't produce income. She had begun working two and three minimum-wage jobs at a time and still never made enough money to keep her head above water. Besides, with that kind of work schedule she'd rarely seen her kids, and she'd hated it that strangers were raising Mindy, Ashley and Donnie.

Her next attempt to pay her own way had been to quit all of her jobs and start a home business. She had shopped yard and garage sales and bought things that she could fix up and sell for a higher price. She had a natural knack for spotting a good piece of furniture hiding beneath layers of old paint, and the best part of that business was that whenever she left the house, her kids could go with her. She made money too, but it wasn't steady money, and after a few months she'd finally had to admit that what she was doing could only be a sideline venture. She *had* to come up with something that brought in money on a regular basis.

By that time her garage was crammed with furniture that needed restoring, and she usually worked at night, after the kids were in bed, finishing pieces that could then be sold. During those quiet hours Gwen had racked her brain for a solution to her financial quandary, and gradually the concept of Help-Mate had taken shape. It had excited her.

Getting the company started had taken time and money; the time she could provide herself, but not the money, and she had approached her parents for a loan. Jack and Lillian Lafferty had thought her idea a good one, and had agreed to loan her the money to get started. Gwen had vowed to pay back every cent her generous parents had ever given or loaned to her, and now, a year later, she was trying very hard to keep that vow. Some of the two thousand that she would receive from Zane Fortune was going to them.

After completing her appointments on that fateful day, Gwen drove to Ramona's house to pick up her kids.

Ramona met her at the door, and her expressive dark eyes became concerned. "Gwen, you look so tired. Come in and sit down for a few minutes. The kids are playing in the backyard and are fine."

Gwen followed her friend to the kitchen, and Ramona brought two glasses of iced tea to the table before asking, "Gwen, is something wrong? You look a little pale around the gills."

Sighing, Gwen took a drink of her tea. "I agreed to do something today that's been bothering me ever since." She stared broodingly out the kitchen window and watched her kids and Ramona's running and playing in the fenced yard. She was incredibly lucky to have found Ramona, and they were both lucky because their kids got along so well.

Ramona sat down and sipped her own tea. Finally she said, "Well, are you going to tell me what you did, or are you going to just sit there and let me die of curiosity?"

That brought a smile to Gwen's lips. Ramona was a very pretty young woman, but like herself, Ramona hadn't dated since her husband's death. They talked about men every so often, though, and both of them felt the same way. Their kids came first, but if some really great guy should stumble into their lives, neither of them was against a second marriage. However, they weren't actively seeking a man, and sometimes they giggled together over some guy's bumbling efforts to make time with one or the other of them.

Gwen was grateful that she had a friend like Ramona, someone in whom she could confide her innermost thoughts. Today she definitely needed to do some confiding.

"I'm sure you recall my mentioning that Zane Fortune is one of my clients," Gwen said quietly.

"Yes. What about it?"

"I met him today."

Ramona's eyes got big. "You did? Is he as good-looking in person as he appears to be in photos?"

"He's even better looking in person. But that's neither here nor there, Ramona. He asked me to do something that..." Gwen frowned, then went on. "He offered me two thousand dollars to attend a wedding with him this weekend."

"You're kidding!" Ramona frowned too. "Why on earth would Zane Fortune have to pay a woman for a date?"

Gwen groaned. "You just hit the nail on the head. I agreed to take money for going out with a man. Ramona, there are names for women who do that."

"Oh, but surely he doesn't expect..." Ramona's voice trailed off, and she weakly added, "Does he?"

"I asked him point-blank what he expected for his money, and he made it sound... Well, let me explain how this all came about." Gwen related the incident with Alamo, then how Zane Fortune had offered her the business deal.

"He said that the most I would have to do was to act a bit love-struck, and maybe hold his hand."

Ramona sat back, appearing dumbfounded. "That is the strangest thing I've ever heard."

"Yes, isn't it?" Gwen agreed. "I asked him why he didn't simply tell his female relatives that he didn't want a wife, and he said that he'd tried but never quite made the grade. Apparently he doesn't want to hurt anyone's feelings. Ramona, I admit that I saw dollar signs when I agreed to his request, and you know how badly I need the money, but would I be selling myself? It's been driving me crazy since the moment I left his house."

Ramona held up her hands. "Let's look at it this way. You're in the service business, and wouldn't this just be another service? Gwen, with his looks, position and money, Zane Fortune could have any woman he wanted. I don't think he would have to pay for any sort of hanky-panky. But if he is one of those men who does pay for it, wouldn't he go to a professional?"

"I...suppose so. Actually, I'm not worried about his motives or morality, I'm worried about mine. Just how far would I go for money? There has to be a point where a decent woman says no. Did I go past that point today by agreeing to accept money for two days of my time?''

"Two days?"

"Yes," Gwen said with another sigh. "It's a two-day wedding party at the Fortunes' Double Crown Ranch. Big doings, apparently. Nothing at all like any event I've ever attended."

"It might be fun," Ramona exclaimed, startling her friend. "Gwen, you haven't done anything just for fun since you lost your husband. I think you should stop worrying, and go to that wedding and enjoy yourself."

"You really feel that way?"

"Yes, I do. Gwen, you know you're a respectable woman and so do I. Apparently Mr. Fortune wants an uninvolved escort, and since he talked about needing an attractive woman to play the part, I think he paid you a very nice compliment. And as you said, you could certainly use the money. I believe that if you turn down his proposal, you'll regret it for a very long time."

"I have thought of that," Gwen said. "Maybe I just needed a pep talk. Usually I'm pretty optimistic and open to new ideas, but this one really threw me for a loop. Are you sure you approve?"

"Of course I approve. Now, let's do something else fun and figure out what clothes you should take with you."

Before they discussed clothes, Gwen needed to ask one more question. "Will you be able to watch my kids for the whole weekend? I'll pay double, Ramona."

"I'll watch the kids and you don't have to pay me double, for heaven's sake. In fact, let's call this weekend a trade-off with no money involved.'' Ramona grinned. "Maybe something exciting will happen to me one of these days, and I'll need a baby-sitter.''

Gwen smiled. "You've got yourself a deal, my friend.''

Gwen was glad she had talked to Ramona about Zane Fortune's proposition. If nothing else, it had made her realize that the issue of her own morality hadn't been the cause of her reluctance at all. She'd never been a Goody Two-shoes, after all. She'd been pregnant when she and Paul got married, which was the reason she hadn't finished college.

So what she had really done, after leaving Zane's home yesterday, was hide her true concerns behind questions about right and wrong. That had been much easier to do than face what had really been bothering her: spending two days with Zane Fortune, meeting his family and friends, and pretending that she and Zane were lovers.

She faced it squarely the next day while getting ready for Zane to pick her up. She had already driven her kids over to Ramona's, each of them with a small overnight bag, then had returned home and started working on herself. It was no small task to turn herself into a lady of some leisure. While she filed and polished her short fingernails, and gave herself a pedicure, she worried about whether she would be able to fool anyone into thinking that a man like Zane Fortune would find a woman like her attractive. And if she were to believe Zane's story to the letter, she was going to be under a lot of scrutiny. From people who were millionaires, yet! Probably not one woman she would meet at that wedding had ever done her own fingernails or given herself a pedicure.

But all that aside, Gwen's biggest worry was Zane himself. He was too good-looking, too rich, too sure of himself. She'd never met anyone even remotely similar before, and there was some part of her that was uncomfortably drawn to the glamorous appeal Zane exuded. Gwen was positive that her pragmatic side would never let her actually fall in love with anyone like Zane Fortune, but was it strong enough to prevent her from developing a silly, futile schoolgirl crush on the man?

She couldn't deny the possibility, and it bothered her so much that she dialed Ramona's phone number. "How are the kids doing?"

"You should be getting ready instead of worrying."

"I am getting ready, but I just realized something. Last night I talked about morality versus money and that wasn't what was eating at me at all. I—I'm afraid of Zane Fortune."

"Oh, God, there's something you didn't tell me. Do you think he's a pervert, or something?"

"Ramona, no!" Gwen was appalled that she'd given her friend such a horribly false impression. "The truth, Ramona, is that I'm going to be spending two days with the most incredible man I've ever met, and what if I...well, end up liking him?"

"Well, think about this," Ramona said wryly, "What if *he* ends up liking you?"

"Oh, he wouldn't! I mean, how could he?"

"For heaven's sake, Gwen, are you deliberately looking for a reason to drive yourself crazy? In the first place you might not like him at all. In the second, why are you so positive that he could never like you?"

"I just know it. Compare his life-style to mine and you'll know it too."

"Because he's rich and you're not? So what? Gwen, I think that what you're really afraid of is meeting his wealthy family and friends. You're as good as any of them, and don't you dare act like you're not."

"What if I can't pull it off?"

"Good grief, you're the most creative person I know. Create a persona for yourself that will knock everyone's socks off, Zane Fortune's included."

Gwen glanced at the two dresses hanging on the closet door that she'd thought would be best for the charade Zane had hired her for; she hadn't yet decided which one to wear for the wedding today. Although they were both pretty dresses, neither of them would knock anyone's socks off.

But she had one in her closet that just might do that. "Create a persona for myself, hmm?" she murmured, more to herself than to Ramona.

"And make it a noticeable one. Now hang up and get to it. I'll be on pins and needles till you get back tomorrow, and you'd better have some darn good stories to tell me."

"'Bye, Ramona," Gwen said absentmindedly, and put down the phone. Hurrying to the closet she took out a plastic bag, then removed the bag and studied the dress it had protected for well over a year. She was pleased to smell no mustiness but rather the faint scent of her favorite perfume; she had dropped several sachets of the fragrance into the bag when she'd put the dress away. Next she reached to the top shelf of the closet for a shoe box, and in it were the stunning high heels that went with the dress.

"You want to impress your family, Mr. Fortune?"

she said under her breath. "Fine, we'll impress your family."

Zane had instructed Gwen to dress for the wedding ceremony and reception afterward, because he would be picking her up just early enough to allow for the drive to the ranch. "Bring an overnight case with whatever else you think you might need. Along with Saturday's big event, there's going to be a Sunday morning brunch. It will be casual, so slacks or even jeans will do for that."

She realized it hadn't even occurred to him that she might not have appropriate clothes for a formal wedding—which didn't surprise her considering how he lived. He was in for at least one surprise.

When she was finally made up, coiffed and dressed, she stared at her own reflection with a feeling of wonder. Was that woman in the mirror really her? It had been so long since she'd worn anything but jeans, shorts and old tops, and just as long since she'd put on makeup and spent time on her hair, that she could hardly believe her own eyes.

Charged up over looking so good, Gwen finished packing her overnight case, and was ready and waiting when her front doorbell chimed. She was carrying her handbag and the small suitcase when she opened the door.

"Hello," she said, and then watched a wash of confusion erase his smile.

"You…you're gorgeous!" he blurted, alerting Gwen to the fact that he hadn't expected her to look as she did.

She smiled. "Save the flattery for later, when we have an audience," she said pertly, and pulled the door closed behind her. Brushing past him, she started down the front steps.

Zane wondered about his almost stupefied reaction to Gwen's appearance. He *never* had trouble talking to women, and compliments had always rolled off his tongue smooth as silk. Blurting was not his style, and yet he had definitely blurted when Gwen opened her door. In fact, he was still amazed at her astonishing transformation from the soggy but pretty woman in his mind to this glamorous creature.

Regaining his wits, he hurried to catch up with Gwen and take the overnight bag from her hand. "I'll put this in the trunk."

"Thank you."

He opened the passenger door of his luxury car and she got in. Because her skirt was split, he caught a glimpse of a long, sensually shaped thigh as she brought her legs around, and a jolting awareness of Gwen Hutton as a highly desirable woman suddenly buffeted Zane. Frowning, he rounded the back of the car, paused to put her bag in the trunk, then continued to the driver's side.

After starting the engine, he looked her way and gave her another amazed once-over. When she turned her head and looked at *him* with a raised eyebrow, he stammered, "Guess I'm staring, huh?"

"I'd say so," Gwen said dryly.

Since stammering was another thing Zane never did with women, his doing so now unnerved him. Gwen appeared to be cool as a cucumber, and he felt like a tongue-tied boy. Unusual, *damn* unusual, he thought uneasily as he pulled away from the curb.

Of course, he hadn't expected her to look like a fashion model, he thought in defense of his behavior.

Her dress was really a stunning black suit with pale gray satin piping around lapels that were just far enough apart to permit a glimpse of cleavage, which was sexier to Zane than if her entire bosom was on display. Her hosiery was gray and her high-heeled pumps were black. Her hair had been piled on top of her head in a mass of curls, with floating tendrils around her face and nape that tormented Zane.

Gripping the steering wheel tightly, he tried to concentrate on driving instead of on the way Gwen looked. But inhaling the subtle scent of her perfume with every breath worked against him, and he kept stealing peeks at her.

Finally, he couldn't keep quiet any longer. "You're going to knock my family out," he said. "My friends too."

"That's what you wanted to accomplish, wasn't it? I mean, isn't this entire charade aimed at impressing your family and friends?"

"True." Zane laughed then, albeit weakly. "Guess I didn't expect to be impressed myself."

Uh-oh, Gwen thought warily. If she let herself, she could be *very* impressed by him. He looked fabulous in his dark suit and white shirt, and she would bet anything that the tie he was wearing had cost as much as her entire outfit—which she'd bought on markdown.

But she had not dressed to impress him, she insisted to herself. She was only keeping up her side of their "business arrangement," and she didn't want to hear any more compliments from him while they were alone.

"Let's keep this strictly impersonal," she said coolly. "I have a few questions. Since you want your family to believe we're a...couple, I should know a little more about you than I do. For instance, how do you take your coffee, and what's your favorite drink as far as alcoholic beverages go?''

"I suppose you're right, but remember that I should know more about you too. Coffee strong and black, and while I'm not much of a drinker, I prefer scotch. What about you?''

"Coffee with cream, no sweetener. Wine or champagne only. Are you a reader?''

"I run in spurts. I doubt if anyone's going to ask you what book I might be in the middle of reading."

"Probably not. I enjoy reading but have little time for it. Same with TV.'' Gwen paused, then asked, "If someone asks me what I do, what would you like me to say?''

Zane sent her a frown. "Is there anything wrong with the truth?''

"Not to me there isn't, but bathing dogs and running other people's errands is hardly a glamorous job.''

"It's an honest living. Just be yourself, Gwen, except for our supposed relationship. Now *that* subject might raise some questions. How we met, for example.''

"Well, if I'm going to be honest about my job, I might as well be honest about that, as well.''

"Might as well be,'' Zane agreed, then chuckled. "It was pretty funny, wasn't it? Your chasing Alamo through the house, both of you sopping wet?''

"Hilarious,'' Gwen said wryly.

"Of course, you can't say it happened only yesterday. I'd like everyone to think that we've been seeing each other for at least two weeks.''

"Fine," Gwen snapped.

Zane sent her a look. "You don't like lying, do you?"

"Never did, never will. But it's what you're paying me for, and I'll do what I can to help you pull the wool over your relatives' eyes."

"When you put it that way, it seems pretty underhanded," Zane muttered.

"It *is* underhanded." Gwen sighed. "But it's your family, and I'm just the hired help."

That last remark hit Zane the wrong way, and he fell silent to stew privately. It was too late to wish he'd met Gwen under different circumstances and hadn't instantly seen her as a replacement for Heather, but the thought was there, all the same. He didn't like Gwen thinking of herself as the "hired help," but what could he do about it now? They were almost to the ranch, and he knew they would be rushed by relatives the minute they arrived. Everyone would want to meet his lady friend; he and Gwen would instantly have to go into their act.

No, there was no turning back now. He was caught in a trap of his own making, and wishing that he'd never thought up this ridiculous scheme was an exercise in futility. He'd forever set the tone of any possible relationship with Gwen Hutton, and he would have to live with it.

Three

Gwen had known she was in for a range of new experiences during this November weekend, but the armed guards at the entrance to the ranch took her completely by surprise.

Zane pulled to a stop and rolled down his window. "Hello, Dan," he said, as one of the guards bent over and peered into the car.

"How are you, Zane?" Dan asked cordially.

"Just fine. Nice day for a wedding."

"That it is." Dan stood away from the car and motioned Zane on.

"What was that all about?" Gwen asked.

"They're just making sure that everyone is an invited guest." Zane paused, then added, "Dad has become very security conscious. It started after Matthew's infant son was kidnapped."

"I recall reading about that. The Fortune name is often in the newspapers."

"It's in the papers too damn often," Zane said gruffly. "That's another reason for those guards at the gate—to keep out the media."

Gwen's next surprise was the valet parking. Young men, smartly dressed in black trousers and red jackets, were parking the arriving guests' vehicles in neat rows in a field of freshly mowed grass.

"Is that huge parking area the norm?"

Zane found himself pleased with Gwen's curiosity. At the same time he hoped that the army of family and friends she would meet this weekend wouldn't overwhelm her. Dressed as she was today she looked sophisticated and confident, but the Fortune family en masse could daunt the strongest spirit, and Zane suspected that Gwen had never attended an affair like this one promised to be. He suddenly felt very protective of her and swore that he would do his best to shield her from some of his nosier relatives.

"For special occasions, yes," he said. He stopped the car at the Valet Parking sign. "We'll get out here."

At last Gwen could see the ranch compound, and she was mesmerized by the sight of Ryan Fortune's sprawling mansion, the huge white wedding tents set on emerald-green grass, the number and variety of flowers that seemed to be everywhere and the mingling crowd of fabulously dressed people.

She was still staring, still attempting to digest everything, when someone opened her door. "Ma'am?" one of the valets said politely, and offered his hand to help her from the car.

She felt a bit dazzled by it all, but she managed to smile at the young man and thank him when she was out of the car and on her feet. Zane was instantly at her side.

"Our luggage will be taken care of," he told her. "Your suitcase will be brought to the bedroom you'll be using tonight." She wore a strange expression, and Zane hoped that her confidence wasn't already slipping. "Are you all right?" he asked.

Gwen lifted her chin. It was true that she wasn't accustomed to such luxurious surroundings, but she'd never been afraid of meeting new people, and that was really all she was going to be doing.

"I'm fine," she said. When he still looked a little uncertain, she added, "Zane, I really am. Stop worrying." She took in a breath. "Shall we get started?"

He offered his arm, grinned and said, "Yes, ma'am."

The first couple to greet them was Dallas and Maggie Fortune. Zane and Dallas shook hands, Zane kissed Maggie's cheek, and said, "Gwen, this is my brother, Dallas, and his wife, Maggie." To his brother and sister-in-law he said, "This beautiful lady is my very special friend, Gwen Hutton."

Gwen saw surprise in both Dallas's and Maggie's eyes, but they shook her hand and smiled warmly. Smiling herself, she murmured, "Very nice meeting you."

That was just the beginning. By the time everyone went into the designated tent for the wedding ceremony, Gwen's head was spinning with names and faces. Not so much that she didn't notice the elegant decorations inside the tent, however. It was all so lovely, so tastefully done, she thought emotionally. She had never pined for great wealth, but from what she'd seen so far today, wealth did have its advantages. If she had to pay for a wedding, for example, it would have none of the glamorous pageantry of this affair. Her thoughts drifted to the future, and she hoped ardently that when the time came for her children to marry she would have the financial means to at least help them pay for a memorable wedding.

She remained emotional throughout the ceremony. The bride was beautiful in a stunning white gown, and the groom was extraordinarily handsome in a formal gray cutaway suit. Their attendants were beautifully attired.

Zane and Gwen had been seated in the second row of chairs, almost directly behind Zane's father, Ryan, and the bride's mother, Lily Cassidy. Gwen was positive she had never met a more beautiful woman than Lily, who possessed an exotic, ageless beauty. Gwen recalled meeting Cole Cassidy, Lily's son, and his fiancée Annie, and then meeting a young woman named Maria Cassidy, who had been standing alone. Was Maria another one of Lily's children? Gwen wondered. If she was, she was very different from the rest of her family. Of course, Gwen reasoned, she hadn't yet met Hannah Cassidy, or rather Hannah Malone, she amended just as the minister said, "I now pronounce you husband and wife."

As the bride and groom kissed, people began rising. Parker and Hannah, arm-in-arm and wearing big smiles, swept down the aisle.

Gwen and Zane stood up. "It was a beautiful wedding," Gwen said huskily, still feeling emotional.

"I think weddings are catching," Zane said with a laugh. "There've been almost a dozen of them among my friends and family in less than two years. Did I tell you I'm the last holdout in the Fortune family?"

"I don't remember your mentioning it," Gwen said rather dryly. "But I knew there had to be a reason why your female relatives believe it's your turn."

"And speaking of my single status, Gwen, you've been doing a great job. I've overheard comments. 'Who is she?' 'How did Zane meet her?' 'She's quite lovely, isn't she?' Things like that. You've got them all talking and wondering." Zane took Gwen's elbow and steered her into the aisle.

"Then I guess I'm earning my pay," Gwen said, deliberately striving to sound a bit sarcastic. She'd been slowly but surely becoming unnerved being with Zane. It was extremely discomfiting to look directly at him, especially into his cobalt-blue eyes. It wasn't just his outstanding good looks that troubled her, either, it was *him!* All of him— his aura, his smile, his voice, his grace of movement. In truth, she could find no flaw in Zane Fortune. He was intelligent, friendly and charming. And he exuded a sex appeal that any woman would have to be totally numb not to feel. It was especially prevalent when he touched her as he was doing now, with a completely innocent hold on her elbow to escort her from the wedding tent.

Gwen wasn't at all numb, and her involuntary reactions to Zane were making her nervous. The second they were outside the tent, she moved her arm just enough to discretely get rid of his hand.

She could see that the mingling had begun again. People were milling, talking and laughing. "Come on," Zane said. "You have to meet the bride and groom."

"Of course," she murmured, and once again he took her elbow, this time to steer her toward the newlyweds. After introductions, Gwen offered congratulations and best wishes. Since others were waiting to do the same, she and Zane didn't linger. But she'd sensed something from Parker Malone that she'd felt with no one else today.

"Does your friend know I'm a paid date?" she asked sharply.

Zane was startled. "Absolutely not! No one knows, and I'd just as soon keep it that way. What made you think Parker knew about our arrangement?"

Gwen felt a little foolish. "Obviously I misunderstood his, uh, scrutiny."

"He's curious, Gwen, same as everyone else. He might be even more curious than most because we're good friends and I never mentioned you to him. Which I couldn't do, of course, since you and I only met yesterday."

"You sound angry. I'm sorry if I upset you."

"I'm not angry. Look, we'll be eating soon. Maybe you'd like to go to your bedroom and freshen up."

Gwen eagerly grasped at the opportunity to be alone for a few minutes. "Yes, I would. How do I find it?"

"There are people in the house directing traffic. Most of the family will be staying overnight. Just tell anyone your name and someone will show you to your room. I'll go over and talk to Dad and Lily while you're gone."

Grateful for his thoughtfulness, Gwen laid a hand on Zane's arm. "Thank you."

Zane grinned. "Maybe I'm not as bad as you thought, huh?"

Gwen flushed. "If I gave you that impression, I apologize. See you later."

Zane walked over to Ryan and Lily. "Great wedding, Lily," he said. "Hannah is very good at her craft."

"Yes, she is," Lily agreed, obviously proud of the career Hannah had built around planning weddings and other special events.

"Zane," Ryan said with a broad, approving smile, "your companion is a lovely girl. Is it serious this time?"

The one person Zane didn't want to lie to was his dad. Lily, with her usual tact, saved him from doing so. "Ryan, darling, why don't we just wait and see?" She smiled at Zane. "We're all very glad you brought Gwen with you today."

"Thanks, Lily. So, when's the big day for the two of you?"

"Shortly after Christmas," Lily replied. "The invitations should be going out in a week or so. Oh, there's Cole and Annie. Cole! Annie!" she called.

In a few minutes there was a small crowd around Ryan and Lily, and Zane slipped away. He peeked into the second large tent and saw the many tables set up for the wedding feast, which he could see was going to be buffet-style. Waiters in white jackets scurried to get everything ready. The long tables of food were already laden, and more was being brought in as Zane watched. There was also a small stage where musicians were preparing to entertain the guests. Zane took note of the cases of champagne, scotch and bourbon stacked behind two different bars as bartenders readied glasses, napkins and cocktail mixes.

Grinning, Zane shook his head. Obviously a Texas-style party was in the making. A *Fortune-style* party, he amended. Sensing someone behind him, he turned to find his sister Vanessa, whom he greeted with a hug.

"How are you, Zane?" Vanessa asked.

"Couldn't be better," he said breezily.

"Your lady friend took everyone by surprise."

"Did she really?"

"I like her, Zane. She seems to fit you."

"You mean that Gwen and I look like a couple?" Zane asked teasingly.

"The two of you strike me that way, yes, but you seem amused by the idea." Vanessa sighed. "Is Gwen just another short-term girlfriend? She appears to be so much more.''

Zane braced himself for an out-and-out lie. "She means a lot to me, Vanessa." But then he saw the sudden hope on his sister's face and quickly added, "Of course, who knows how long that will last? Personal relationships are such damnably unpredictable things."

Vanessa looked disappointed. "Your relationships have been very predictable, Zane, which I find terribly sad."

"Sad! Sis, there's nothing sad about my life-style."

"Since I'm on the outside looking in, I'll have to take your word for it. But, Zane, when you finally fall in love—I mean *really* fall in love—then you'll realize what you've been missing by flitting from woman to woman."

Zane laughed with genuine relish. "I guarantee that I haven't been missing much, old girl."

Vanessa couldn't help laughing too. "Don't you 'old girl' me, Zane Fortune! You're four years older than I am, and don't you forget it."

While Zane and Vanessa teased each other and laughed together, Gwen enjoyed the silence of the lovely bedroom to which she'd been shown. As Zane had predicted, her suitcase had been brought up, and she unpacked her things. The room had a private bathroom, and the two rooms were decorated in a delicate lemony color.

Gwen wished she could stay in that lovely suite for the rest of the day, but of course that wasn't an option. She had to earn that two-thousand dollars; Zane certainly wouldn't pay her that sum if she hid in her bedroom. Dinner was still to come, then dancing and partying until a supper was served at midnight. The best Gwen could hope for was that Zane would call it a day long before the midnight meal.

Sighing, she washed her hands at the sink and took stock of her face in the mirror above it. Her hairdo was still in place and her makeup was fine, except for her lipstick which took about five seconds to refresh.

She brushed small specks from her stylish black suit and was glad she'd worn it. She'd noticed quite a few women wearing black today, and had, in fact, received several compliments on her outfit.

Thus far, she felt that she had fielded questions about Zane and herself quite well. There'd been a lot more curious looks than outright questions, she realized, and if that pattern continued she wouldn't have to relate any detailed stories about how they'd met and how long they had known each other.

Of course, right now she didn't know which was worse—lying or telling the truth. If she was honest with herself, she could not deny that she was exceptionally attracted to Zane—and becoming more so with every minute they pretended to be a couple. But she didn't try to kid herself about how he might feel about her. Their arrangement was business and nothing more. Tomorrow he would pay her, and other than the off-chance of running into each other when she went to his house to bathe Alamo or to take care of other chores, they would never see each other again.

The thing that seemed so unfair about it all was that she had not been even slightly attracted to another man since her widowhood. Why her hormones should suddenly come to life over Zane Fortune, a man she could never have, was an annoying mystery. He was a Fortune, and she was…well, what was she, other than a woman alone who struggled daily to feed and clothe her children? Yes, she could dress herself up as she'd done today and put on a pretty good show of sophistication, but down deep she wasn't a bit sophisticated. She was ordinary—very, very ordinary—and Zane Fortune was anything but.

It was time she returned to the party, and Gwen left the bedroom. She said a pleasant hello to everyone she saw as she made her way through Ryan's fabulous home to reach the same door through which she'd entered the mansion.

A short plump woman with a lovely silver streak in her black hair approached her. "Hello. You're Zane's friend, Gwen Hutton. I'm Rosita Perez. You probably met my daughter Maggie. She's married to Dallas."

"Why yes, I did meet Maggie." Gwen offered her hand for a handshake, and Rosita Perez took it in both of hers, startling Gwen into a stammer. "It's, uh, very nice meeting you, Mrs. Perez."

"Call me Rosita," she said as she turned Gwen's hand over and peered at her palm. "Ah, yes, just as I suspected."

"You suspected what?" Gwen said cautiously. Was this woman a little light in the upper story, or what?

"You're in love," Rosita said calmly. "And you will be married right after the new year. What's this I see? Children! How wonderful! You and Zane will have four children."

Gwen yanked her hand back. "Mrs. Perez, everything you think you saw in my hand is as far from the truth as it could get. Now, if you'll excuse me?"

"You're quite wrong, my dear," Rosita called out cheerfully as Gwen hastened away.

Outside, Gwen tried to calm her shaken system with breaths of fresh air. Without a doubt Rosita Perez was the strangest person she'd met here today. Zane's relatives might be curious about his latest girlfriend, but at least they were polite about it.

Latest girlfriend? Gwen's spirits dropped another notch. She was a *hired* girlfriend, and she had better not forget it for even a moment!

In the next heartbeat she saw Zane walking toward her. Apparently he'd been watching for her. How was she going to get through the rest of today and then tomorrow morning with him being so consistently attentive, when she couldn't seem to rid herself of feelings for the man that just kept going deeper?

Well, she had to do it, that was all there was to it. She had to smile and talk and act as though he wasn't the most incredible guy she'd ever met. Inwardly she groaned. Why was this happening to her?

Zane walked up to her and smiled. "Is your room satisfactory?"

"It's a lovely room. Zane, I met the strangest woman in the house. She's Maggie's mother, Rosita, and when I offered to shake her hand, she took mine and read my palm."

Zane let out a whoop of laughter. "So you met our local oracle."

Gwen's jaw dropped. "Are you saying she's a genuine soothsayer?"

"I'm only saying this, Gwen. Rosita Perez has accurately predicted many an event, and folks around here have come to respect her predictions."

"You don't mean it," Gwen said weakly.

"What did she see in your palm?"

"Uh, I'd rather not say. I don't believe in that foolishness, anyhow, so it doesn't matter what she told me.''

"Really," Zane said with a small chuckle. "Know what I think? I think Rosita told you something that shook your underpinnings, and you wish she hadn't. Come on, be a sport and tell me what she said."

"Think what you want. I'm still not telling you what she said to me.". Gwen noticed people filing into the second tent. "Shall we join the others?"

Zane nodded amiably, but he would have given almost anything to know what Rosita had told Gwen. Maybe he could pry it out of Rosita, but he'd much rather hear it from Gwen.

As they strolled toward the dinner tent, he realized how much he was enjoying the day. And his enjoyment was mostly thanks to Gwen. That was food for thought—some very pleasant thought, he discovered.

Throughout the meal people kept rising and offering toasts to the newlyweds. Gwen's—and everyone else's—champagne glass was filled again and again. Gwen became more mellow and relaxed with each swallow she took of the most delicious champagne she'd ever tasted. She realized, if a bit fuzzily, that she was truly enjoying herself. It was becoming much easier to smile at Zane, and even to flirt with him. It was, in fact, almost possible to forget that she was being paid to flirt with him for the benefit of his female relatives, and to pretend that this was a real date.

When he laid his arm across the back of her chair, she smiled and leaned his way. He whispered in her ear, "This is great. I'd bet anything that a good half of my family is wondering when *our* wedding is going to take place."

"Right after the new year," Gwen murmured dreamily.

"Pardon? I didn't catch that."

Gwen felt heat in her face. "Uh, it was nothing." How could she have repeated Rosita's prediction so carelessly? It certainly was not going to come true, for pity's sake. *Watch yourself, Gwen Hutton!*

The bride and groom got up to dance the first dance, and soon others were dancing as well. Zane talked quietly, for Gwen's ears alone. "I should dance with you first, then do a little circulating."

"Whatever you say."

A few minutes later she was on the dance floor with Zane, and he was holding her as a lover held a woman. It had been a long time since Gwen had done any dancing, especially *this* kind of dancing, and she unconsciously stroked the back of Zane's neck as they floated around the dance floor, all but glued together.

The intimate caress startled Zane for a moment, but then he told himself that Gwen was merely putting on a good act. Rationalizing didn't stop his body from responding, however, and he brought her closer still and deliberately inhaled her arousing scent. However this whole thing had started out with Gwen, business deal or not, he knew now that he wanted her. She hadn't only impressed his family and friends today, she had impressed him.

"You're very beautiful," he whispered.

"Thank you, kind sir. You're beautiful too, you know," she said teasingly.

"You think I'm still pretending, Gwen, but I'm not. You really are beautiful."

The hoarseness in his voice jolted Gwen a bit, but

she could only think that if he wasn't pretending at this moment, then he was handing her a line.

"I know all about your reputation with women," she whispered, "so please don't insult me with false flattery just because we both drank too much champagne."

For a few seconds Zane was at a loss. He certainly hadn't expected that sort of reply, and it hurt that she would bring up his reputation at a time like this.

"Don't you recognize a sincere compliment when you hear one?" he finally asked.

"Yes, I believe I do."

"Meaning you don't believe in *my* sincerity."

"That sounds about right." The music had stopped and they had stopped dancing, but Zane kept holding her. She tilted her head back to see his face and was rather surprised by his frowning expression. "Right now you are getting exactly what you wanted from today. People are watching," she said, adding, "A *lot* of people. You really should erase that frown or they'll think we just had a disagreement."

"Right now I don't give a damn what anyone thinks," Zane growled. "Except for you."

"Why would it matter to you what I thought about anything?"

"That's a damn good question and maybe it's something we should *both* think about." Releasing his hold on her, he took her hand and led her back to their table. When she was seated, he leaned over and said, "I'm going to dance with Lily and my sisters. Will you be all right?"

"Of course I'll be all right," she stated confidently, but after he'd gone she sucked in the breath she needed very badly and told her racing pulse to calm down. Without question Zane had come on to her. She'd imagined all sorts of things happening today and this evening, but not that. And the turmoil in her system because of a few words of phony flattery scared the daylights out of her.

What scared her even more, though, were her own reactions to Zane Fortune. Whatever had made her think that she would be impervious to the famous Fortune charm?

Four

Gwen left the tent to avoid having to dance with someone else while Zane was away. Instead of going to the house and to her bedroom, as she would have liked to do, Gwen sat just outside the tent on a lawn chair. The sounds of music, merry laughter and a hundred conversations caused Gwen to heave a sigh. The disparity in the life-styles of the very rich and people like herself suddenly seemed more conspicuous than it had all day. Obviously she'd been so caught up in pretense that she'd believed her own charade. And it had been fun for a while being all dressed up and socializing with the upper crust. Yes, she'd had moments of genuine enjoyment today.

But then reality—*her* reality—had returned. Zane Fortune making a pass—or rather, handing her a line—had brought her back to earth.

Gwen wished he hadn't done that. Other than a few strained moments, they had gotten along quite well all day, and now she felt as though she was no more than the most current entry on his list of 'Possible Conquests.' She was not going to advance to the 'Conquest' list, no matter how handsome, charming and downright sexy he was. And Zane was those things and more, she thought miserably. Why couldn't she find a man of her own class who could knock her dead with a smile and then bring her back to life by simply breathing in her ear?

There's no such person, you romantic fool! Even Zane Fortune isn't Prince Charming.

"But he's close," Gwen mumbled under her breath.

"There you are." Zane pulled a lawn chair over to the one Gwen was using and sat next to her. "I saw you leave, but I thought you only wanted a breath of cool air and would come back in a minute or so. Are you tired, Gwen? Would you like to call it a day?"

Would I ever! "I am tired, Zane," she said evenly. "Would leaving before the party is over insult anyone?"

Zane chuckled. "That party could go on until dawn. Oh, you didn't get to see Parker and Hannah's departure. She threw her bouquet directly at her mother. Lily couldn't have missed catching it if she'd tried."

"Well, apparently she's going to be the next bride in the family, so it was sweet of Hannah to toss Lily her bouquet." After a pause, Gwen added, "Hannah and Parker seem perfect together."

"They do now, but they went through a lot to reach this stage."

"I guess true love rarely runs smoothly. Isn't that what the poets say?"

"Something to that effect. I'm going to go back in and say good-night to Dad and Lily. I'll only be a minute. Don't move." Zane was on his feet and gone in a flash.

He's a kind, considerate man with extremely good manners. Gwen sighed, wishing she could pinpoint at least one flaw in Zane's character or personality. Then she pondered his reputation with women and decided that could be a flaw.

But it could also be an advantage, depending on which gender was analyzing it. Men undoubtedly admired Zane's prowess with the opposite sex, while women...? Darn, Gwen thought uneasily, women probably admired it too. At least they might until he left them with a broken heart.

You're becoming much too interested in Zane Fortune's love life. Think of something else!

Gwen tried to follow that sensible advice, and was considering next week's work schedule in a relatively relaxed position, with her eyes shut, when she heard footsteps. Thinking that Zane had returned, she opened her eyes. Maria Cassidy was standing in front of her.

For some reason a chill went up Gwen's spine, but she said calmly, "Hello, Maria. Are you enjoying the reception?"

"It's just another excuse for the Fortunes to flaunt their wealth," Maria said with a bitter twist of her lips. Without invitation she plopped down in the chair Zane had used. "How'd you meet Zane?"

Gwen was so uncomfortable with this peculiar young woman that she wished Zane would hurry up and get back.

"Through my work," she said slowly, though she had no intention of explaining details to Maria.

"I hope you know that he has a lot of girlfriends. It would be really stupid of you to think you're the only woman in his life," Maria said with a malevolent little smile.

What maliciousness! Gwen thought, shrinking internally from Maria and wishing again that Zane would return. How on earth did Lily, who was a lady in every sense of the word, have a daughter like Maria? Especially when Lily's other daughter, Hannah, was so much like her mother. What had gone wrong with Maria?

"I know Zane has women friends," Gwen said cautiously.

Maria let out a snort. "Friends, my eye. Obviously you didn't get my meaning. Maybe you *are* stupid!"

Gwen was suddenly furious. How dare this vulgar, mean-minded woman speak to her like this? Forgetting that Zane was due back at any moment, she got to her feet.

How she managed to speak at normal pitch when she was so steaming mad Gwen would never know, but she said quite calmly, "I'm going to say goodnight, Maria," and she walked off. When she heard Maria giggling behind her, she walked faster. That awful young woman had deliberately antagonized her and was now laughing about it!

When Gwen reached the house, she stopped before going in and looked back at the tent. Zane must have been held up, she thought, not at all upset by it. As long as he didn't care that *she* had deserted the party, he could stay up all night. She went into the house and then made her way to her assigned bedroom.

There was a lamp burning, and someone had turned down the bed. The room looked cozy and comfortable. Gwen took off her jacket and skirt and hung them in the closet. The rest of her things went into a bag she'd brought along for used clothing, and finally she pulled her short, silky nightgown over her head. Barefoot and yawning, she went into the bathroom, where she brushed her teeth and removed the pins holding her fancy hair style together. She was giving her long hair a good brushing when someone rapped on the bedroom door.

"Just a moment," she called. She ran for the matching robe she'd left in the bureau drawer, then slipped it on and hurried to open the door. It was Zane, of course. She'd expected it would be. "Sorry I left without talking to you," she said quickly. "But Maria Cassidy cornered me and was saying some terrible things. I really couldn't sit there any longer without losing my temper and batting her one. What is wrong with that woman?"

"What was she saying?" Zane was much more interested in how pretty Gwen looked with her hair down and wearing a lavender silky robe than he was in anything Maria might have said, but he realized that he would discuss any topic to keep this luscious lady talking to him.

Gwen cocked a somewhat cynical eyebrow. "Are you sure you want to know?"

Zane caught on and frowned. "She talked about me? Why on earth would Maria talk about me?"

"I have no idea why Maria would do anything. She strikes me as being a pickle short of a full barrel, Zane."

Zane looked around. "We shouldn't be talking in the hall. Some people might be trying to sleep. Could I come in for a few minutes?"

Gwen hesitated, but gave in quickly with a nonchalant shrug. "Sure, why not?"

Zane stepped into the room and quietly closed the door behind him. "Getting back to Maria, Lily has been worried about her."

"I would imagine she has." Gwen set the hairbrush on the bureau. "Maria seems to have some sort of animosity toward your family. I find that curious, when her mother is engaged to your father."

"It is curious." Zane grinned. "But then I never promised that you wouldn't meet a few odd ducks today. Probably every big family has 'em."

Gwen smiled. "I'm sure you're right." She was certain that Zane was heading for the door when he started walking, and that he would say good-night at any moment. She was stunned when he was suddenly standing about two inches away from her. Her eyes widened when he began toying with her hair, brushing it back from her cheek and winding a curl around his forefinger.

"Wha-what are you doing?" She knew that she sounded breathless, but was it any wonder, when her heart was pounding so hard?

"Something I've wanted to do all day." Zane cupped her face with both of his hands and pressed his lips to hers.

Gwen's entire system went wild with erotic little stirrings. She felt as though her insides were melting and blending together as his mouth possessed and teased hers. It had been too long since she'd been kissed, especially in the way Zane was kissing her, and she honestly did not have the strength of will to push him away.

He smelled heavenly. Oh, yes, she had noticed the incredible scent he wore, besides being aware of his extraordinary good looks, throughout the whole day. Was there a woman alive who wouldn't want to be kissed by Zane Fortune?

But a kiss was one thing and his hands under her nightgown was something else. Gasping for air, Gwen backed up a step. "You're going too far," she said hoarsely.

Zane didn't argue. "You're right. I only intended

to kiss you. I guess I didn't expect to feel such fireworks.''

Gwen saw how flushed his face was and knew that his high color was not caused by embarrassment. He was aroused!

Well, so was she. So much for all that gibberish she'd thought about eluding his 'Conquest' lists. All Zane had had to do was touch her with that special light in his eyes and she'd turned into molten jelly!

''I...I think you'd better go,'' she stammered, while some crazy part of her wished that she had the guts to go for it, to ask him to stay, or even to let him know with the right kind of smile that she didn't want him to go. One night of very hot lovemaking? Oh, yes, didn't every woman deserve to meet a Zane Fortune once in her life?

''Yeah, you're right.'' Zane moved to the door and put his hand on the knob. Then he looked at her. ''Gwen Hutton, you are one very special lady. Good night.''

Brunch was served on the south patio of the house close to noon the next day, and Gwen realized that she was strictly in the company of members of the Fortune family. Apparently the other guests had made their departure sometime between the party last night and brunch today.

It would be very easy to sincerely like these people, Gwen thought about halfway through the meal. Certainly they were all charming to her, all seemingly doing their best to make her feel at ease.

There was nothing in Zane's eyes today except good humor. Nothing at all about that kiss last night. Inwardly she heaved a sigh, and wondered why she felt as though some great and profound chapter of her life had been abruptly and prematurely closed. A kiss meant nothing to Zane, obviously, and it should mean nothing to her. She should thank her lucky stars that Zane had already forgotten it.

When the meal was over and people began rising to leave and bid each other goodbye, most of them made a special effort to tell Gwen how much they had enjoyed meeting her, and that they hoped to see her again soon. She said thank you a dozen times, discovering that she truly meant it. Every one of the Fortunes and their spouses had been kind and pleasant to her. Zane was lucky to have such a wonderful family.

When they started the drive back to San Antonio, Gwen told him exactly that. "I'm going home with a much different impression of the Fortune family than the preconceived notions I arrived with," she said.

"You probably thought we were a bunch of snobs," Zane said with a laugh.

"I think I judged the Fortunes on what I read in the society pages," Gwen said matter-of-factly.

"Without knowing even one of us, do you think you should have judged us at all?"

Gwen felt her face burning. How neatly he had put her in her place.

When Zane pulled into Gwen's driveway, he realized that he had barely noticed her house yesterday. It was an unpretentious little white frame house with green trim, several large shade trees and a fenced yard—very much like all the other homes in the obviously blue-collar neighborhood.

Gwen's garage door was down, and Zane spotted a rather dilapidated white van parked *next* to the garage. "Who drives the van?" he asked.

"I do. I park out there because the garage is full of furniture."

Zane laughed curiously. "Furniture?"

"Yes, I refinish old pieces in my spare time." Gwen was concerned about how to approach the subject of payment. Did Zane have a check with him, or would he put her off with some comment about having a check mailed to her? This part of their arrangement embarrassed and unnerved her. Besides, now that she'd met the Fortune family, she regretted having taken part in Zane's charade. Receiving money for deceiving such nice people made her feel she'd hit an all-time low.

"Speaking of spare time," Zane said with a warm smile, "how about having dinner with me some night this coming week?"

Gwen was dumbfounded. Those were positively the last words she could have imagined coming out of Zane's mouth. She could think of only one reason why he would want to see her again. His sexual appetite had been whetted by that kiss last night, and what she really was requesting was another opportunity to get her into bed.

"Sorry," she said coolly, "but I don't date."

"Not at all?" It was Zane's turn to look dumbfounded. "Uh, do you have a reason for not dating?"

"Dozens," she said flatly. "Now, if you'll get my suitcase from the trunk, I'll let you be on your way."

Perplexed, Zane kept looking at her. "I guess I don't understand. You don't *ever* date?"

"I haven't dated since my husband's death."

"You're a widow? Damn, Gwen, I'm really sorry. For some reason I thought you were a single woman. Well, you are, of course, but—"

"I know what you meant." Gwen did know. What she didn't know was why she hadn't told Zane about her widowhood before this. And she hadn't mentioned her three kids, either. That was something else he should know. He would probably retract his dinner invitation so fast that her head would spin.

She was about to surprise him with that bit of news when he reached across her and opened the glove compartment. Taking out an envelope, he handed it to her.

Warily Gwen lifted the flap and saw a sheaf of one-hundred dollar bills. He'd paid her in cash. She suddenly felt like bawling.

"You did a great job this weekend," Zane said.

"Please get my suitcase," she said hoarsely, only holding back the urge to cry through sheer willpower.

"Right away." Zane pushed a button that opened the trunk, then got out of the car.

Before he could open her door, Gwen got out too. Taking the suitcase from his hand, she said without looking at him, "I'll bring this in the house, then go and pick up my kids."

Zane soberly studied her profile. "I didn't know you were a widow, I didn't know you had kids. How come, Gwen? When we were talking about knowing enough about each other to fool my family, why didn't you mention having kids?"

"Since they're my entire life, I honestly don't know. Goodbye, Zane." Turning, Gwen walked to the front door of the house, unlocked it and went in.

Zane didn't ask one question about your kids, not how many you have or how old they are. He puts on a great show of good manners and kindly consideration, but deep down, where it counts, he's really as

self-centered as they come. Thank goodness you didn't
do something foolish with him last night, something
you'd be painfully regretting today.

Sighing, Gwen changed from the good slacks she'd
worn for brunch into a pair of faded jeans and a cotton
sweater. Obviously her having kids had diluted Zane's
interest, which shouldn't surprise her in the least. Besides, it was just as well, she told herself. He'd shaken
her up this weekend, and she didn't need that sort of
nonsense in her busy life.

Within ten minutes of getting home Gwen was
ready to leave again. Hopping into her van, she drove
straight to Ramona's house.

Ramona opened the door for her, looking pleasantly
surprised. "You're back earlier than I expected."

Before Gwen could answer, her kids ran at her full
tilt. Laughing, she got down on her knees and hugged
all three of them at the same time. Kissing their little
faces, she said, "I sure missed you guys."

Donnie, who was five and the oldest, said, "We
watched a movie last night, and Ramona made popcorn."

"With lots of butter," four-year-old Ashley said.
"It was yummy."

Mindy, who was a few months past two, parroted
her sister. "Wots of butter, Mommy."

"Mom, did you ride a horse?" Donnie asked.

Gwen got to her feet. "No, son. I went to a beautiful
ranch, but it was for a wedding, not a horseback ride."

"Aw, heck," Donnie said, sounding disappointed.

Ramona's two kids were standing nearby, and
Gwen smiled at them. Tommy was Donnie's age, and
Liselle was four, like Ashley. Tiny Mindy was a tag-
along, usually following her big sister, whom she

adored and mimicked. Gwen's three were towheads, blond like their father had been, and Ramona's two had dark hair and eyes like herself.

Gwen looked at Ramona. "They're all so adorable I could cry." To her surprise tears filled her eyes. "I could cry" had just been a figure of speech, or so she'd thought. She tried to laugh it off. "Goodness, I seem to be emotional today."

"Yes, you do," Ramona agreed quietly. "Come to the kitchen. I think we need to talk. Kids, you may play outside or in the family room." The children opted for the backyard, and took off running.

Ramona led the way to her kitchen. "Sit at the table, Gwen. Would you like a cup of coffee? It would only take a few minutes to make a pot."

"No, please don't go to any trouble. I'm not going to stay long, Ramona. I have a dozen things to do at home." Gwen took a stab at a smile and knew it came off as feeble.

"Water, then? Or a soda?"

"Just water, thanks."

Ramona brought two glasses of water to the table and sat directly across from Gwen. "You know you can talk to me about anything, Gwen."

"I know."

"So what's bothering you? Was the weekend horrible?"

"No, it wasn't horrible. Quite the opposite, for the most part. I…guess I didn't expect the Fortunes to be nice people, and they are. Zane paid me the two-thousand in cash, and I felt…" A frown creased Gwen's forehead. "When he handed me that money I wished I were in a financial position to refuse it. I was such a fraud with his family and friends, Ramona, and I'm not used to being anyone but myself."

"You're feeling guilty."

"Very," Gwen said sadly. Sighing, she got up without even having sipped her water. "I'm going to gather my brood and go home, Ramona."

Ramona looked disappointed. "I was hoping to hear some details of the wedding, and how you got along with Zane."

Gwen sighed again. "I know you were, and I promise to tell you everything. But not right now, Ramona. Please understand, all I want to do now is take my kids, go home and try to settle my nerves. I need to get back into my own routine, in my own little house. I saw such opulence this weekend that nothing I have seems to have any value. I've got to get back on my own track."

Nodding empathetically, Ramona got up. "If you feel up to it later on, call me."

"Yes, I'll do that."

Within an hour of being in her own home with her kids, Gwen started feeling better. She made macaroni-and-cheese and hot dogs for supper, and she and her little family enjoyed the simple meal. The kids' childish chatter while they ate sounded like music to Gwen's ears. This was her reality, and it was beyond value.

Zane wondered why he was so on edge as he wandered the rooms of his house that evening. The weekend had gone remarkably well. His scheme had worked perfectly, so why didn't he feel good about it? Certainly he felt no remorse over protecting himself from the determined matchmaking of his sisters and sisters-in-law. No, the gnawing sensation in the pit of his stomach had something to do with Gwen. The truth, he finally had to admit, was that he wished he had not involved Gwen Hutton in his little game.

Gwen was like no woman he'd met before. He'd dated widows but never any with children. Then again, had he really gotten to know even one of the women he'd wined, dined and romanced since Melanie Wilson's cataclysmic rejection? It was entirely possible that he hadn't given any woman the chance to talk about her family.

Zane tried defending to himself his sometimes hot, but never sincere, relationships with women by dredging up the pain he'd suffered over Melanie's desertion, and he vowed once more never to put himself through that again. But that all seemed so unconnected to Gwen. It was as though Gwen Hutton stood alone and separate from other women, an independent spirit, a tormenting delight when wearing a wet T-shirt, a tantalizing glamour girl in sophisticated clothing.

After several restless hours of soul-searching, Zane could no longer avoid the truth: he wanted to see Gwen again.

But just how did a man ''see'' a woman who didn't date? He'd never heard of such a thing, he thought in frustration. How could Gwen have *dozens* of reasons for not dating? It had to be an exaggeration, and there was only one reason why she would overstate her feelings about not dating: She did not want to see *him* again.

That conclusion was shocking for Zane. Women *always* wanted to see him again. How many times had he changed his phone number to avoid some determined woman's incessant calls? But he knew in his soul that Gwen would not call. And what would she do if he phoned her? Hang up in his ear, or make polite excuses?

Should he call her and find out? Zane approached the telephone warily, then remembered that he didn't know her home phone number. For that matter, he didn't know her business phone number.

Locating a telephone book, he easily found a G. Hutton with a street address. Sitting back in his chair, he stared at the phone with a knot in his gut. Was he going to call her, or wasn't he?

Fifteen minutes later he reached for the phone and punched out her number.

After dialing Gwen's number a good dozen times and getting a busy signal, Zane slammed the phone down in frustration. Now, just who would she be talking to for so long? It had to be a man, he decided with a dark scowl. She'd out and out lied about not doing any dating.

"To hell with it," he muttered, and got up and went to his bedroom to retire for the night.

Five

Zane put in a busy morning at the office on Monday. Heather was back—her mother was doing fine—and she orchestrated Zane's meetings and phone calls with her usual efficiency.

Around two in the afternoon he had time to think about Gwen and he dialed her home number. He got her answering machine, and when he dialed her business number, he also got an answering machine. He left no messages.

Around three, Heather's voice came over the intercom. "Zane, your sister Vanessa is on line five. Are you able to take the call now, or would you like me to tell her that you will call her back?"

Zane stiffened. Something told him that Vanessa wanted to discuss Gwen, and he did not want to talk about Gwen with anyone. Especially with his matchmaking sister. But Vanessa was tenacious, and sooner or later he would have to have this conversation. He figured he might as well get it over with.

"I'll talk to her, Heather. Thanks." Hitting the button for line five, Zane picked up the phone. "Hello, Vanessa."

"How are you today, Zane?" Vanessa asked warmly.

"Couldn't be better. And you?"

"Just great, thanks. I know you're busy, so I'll get

right to the point. Devin and I were both quite taken with Gwen over the weekend, and we'd like you to bring her to dinner on Wednesday so we can all get better acquainted.''

Zane shook his head disgustedly. No matter what he did there was no escaping his family's determination to marry him off.

"Vanessa, I can't accept an invitation for Gwen without talking to her about it.''

"How about letting me talk to her? I'd love to phone her.''

Zane's heart skipped a suddenly nervous beat. "I'd rather do it myself, if you don't mind. Besides, I'm not sure of my own schedule. Hold on while I check my appointment book.'' Zane saw at once that Wednesday night was open, and his mind raced through his options. It irritated him that he hadn't fore-seen Vanessa or another of his female relatives going into matchmaking overdrive if they liked Gwen. It was quite likely that his weekend scheme had backfired on him—in more ways than one.

For one thing, *he* liked Gwen, which he certainly hadn't expected when he'd proposed his plan to her at his house last Friday. He liked her and wanted to see her again, and he'd had no luck at all in reaching her by telephone.

"Uh, Vanessa, I might be able to make it, but before I make any promises, let me talk to Gwen. I'll get back to you.''

"Of course,'' Vanessa readily agreed. "Call me as soon as you know for sure, one way or the other.''

"I'll do that.''

After goodbyes, Zane hung up, then sat there pon-dering the can of worms he'd opened by introducing

Gwen to his family and deliberately acting as though
she was special to him. It had seemed like a good plan
originally. Now, in retrospect, he could see that it had
been a damn foolish game to be playing. He had half
a notion to call Vanessa back right now and tell her
the whole story.

Instead, he heaved a long sigh and dialed Gwen's
home number again. He got her answering machine.
Same with her business number. Frustrated, he jumped
up, grabbed his suit jacket and left his office. Striding
past Heather's desk he said brusquely, "I'll be gone
about an hour."

He got in his car and drove to Gwen's house. Pulling into her driveway he saw that the parking space
next to the garage was vacant; Gwen's white van was
gone. Damn, he thought impatiently. He knew of no
way to find her. Turning off the ignition, he sat there
and scowled at the front of her house while wondering
what in heck was going on with him. He could have
easily concocted a tale for Vanessa. *Gwen and I broke
up. I won't be seeing her again.* Instead, he'd dug
himself into a deeper hole by letting Vanessa continue
to believe that he and Gwen were a couple.

Obviously he hadn't *wanted* to "break up" with
Gwen.

Zane rubbed the back of his neck while he tried to
find some sense in his own thoughts. He was behaving
as though he and Gwen really *were* a couple. This was
getting weird.

Well, it seemed the only way for him to talk to her
was to sit and wait until she got home.

Gwen was heading for home. Her work schedule
for Help-Mate was finished for the day, and she was

going to pick up a delightful little spindly-legged table she had refurbished, then deliver it to its new owner. She was thinking of a dozen different things as she approached her driveway, which was blocked from view by her neighbor's high hedge, and she made the turn on automatic pilot.

The sight of Zane's car parked in her driveway came as a shock, and she slammed on the brakes and spun the steering wheel to the right. But she'd known the second she'd seen the car that she was going to crash into it, and she did. The left front end of her van connected with the right rear section of Zane's car, bounced off it, then hit it again. The van's engine died, and Gwen groaned in utter disbelief and laid her head on the steering wheel. Dammit! Why had Zane been parked in her driveway, anyway?

Zane unhooked his seat belt, leaped out of his car and ran over to the van. Seeing Gwen's head on the steering wheel made his pulse go wild. She must be injured!

He couldn't open the driver's door because that side of the van was up against the back of his car, so he ran around to the passenger door, yanked it open and climbed in. "Gwen, my God, can you hear me?" he asked frantically.

She raised her head and gave him a murderous look. "Of course I can hear you. What are you doing here? Dammit, now I have an accident to contend with. Why were you parked in my driveway?"

Her anger was so completely unfair that Zane felt a rising anger himself. "Do you always turn in to your driveway at fifty miles an hour?"

"I wasn't going fifty! Good grief," she said scornfully, "a professional driver couldn't make that turn at fifty miles an hour."

"All right, so I exaggerated, but didn't you see my car *before* you turned?" Silently Gwen pointed, and Zane looked to see what she was pointing at. "Oh, the hedge. Well, since neither of us was injured, I guess no real damage was done."

"I can see the damage to your car from here. A few more dents in this old van will hardly be noticed, but I doubt if you're going to ignore *your* dents." *There goes your two-thousand. Good thing you didn't spend it today.* "I'll pay for the repairs, of course," she added dully.

"Your auto insurance should cover it."

"I don't have any auto insurance."

"But you have to carry vehicle insurance. It's the law."

"Is it really?" she drawled.

"You told me you were bonded and licensed to do business as Help-Mate. Now you're saying that you drive this uninsured van onto your clients' property? That's taking a mighty big chance, Gwen. I recommend that you get some vehicle insurance immediately."

"You think you have all the answers and the truth is that you have no idea what you're even talking about." Gwen reached for the ignition key and turned it. When the engine started, she breathed a sigh of relief. The van might be a little more bruised than it had been, but as long as it ran she could deal with its disreputable appearance. She backed it into the street and parked at the curb.

"What do you mean, I don't know what I'm talking about?"

"Leave it alone, Zane," she said wearily. "You couldn't understand the way I live in a million years." She opened her door, got out and walked over to Zane's car. Naturally it was one of the most costly cars on the market, and repairing its back end was not going to be cheap. She heaved a sigh, which she cut short when Zane walked up.

Her gaze flicked over his custom-made suit, shirt and shoes. But it didn't matter that the clothes on his back today had probably cost more than every stitch in her closet. She'd run into his car, and the repairs were her responsibility.

"Get it fixed," she said flatly. "Send me the bill. Now, if you'll move your car so I can get into my garage, I have a table to pick up and deliver."

Zane narrowed his eyes on her. She had a way of asserting her independence that grated on his nerves. It was almost as though she was daring him to step on her pride. Fine, he thought, he wouldn't argue about who was going to pay for the repairs to his car. She would never know which body shop had done the work, and therefore she couldn't pay any part of the bill.

Signs of her way of life were everywhere he looked—her old beat-up van, her small house, and even the harried look in her eyes. Money was probably a constant worry. No wonder she'd taken him up on his offer of two-thousand dollars for spending the weekend at the ranch and pretending that she was his girlfriend.

"I'll move my car in a minute. There's something I have to ask you first. I would have done this on the phone, but you never *answer* the phone."

"I can't sit around the house waiting for the phone to ring. I have to earn a living."

"I know that." Zane found himself speaking gently. Any previous anger he'd felt was gone. There was nothing he'd like more than to write Gwen a large check on the spot. She shouldn't have to struggle to earn a living when he had ten times, twenty times, more money than he could spend in his lifetime. He could well afford to help a friend.

But something told him that the quickest way to forever end his and Gwen's relationship was to try to give her money. He would mull it over; there had to be a way to help her out financially.

"Gwen, my sister Vanessa called and invited you and me to dinner at her house on Wednesday."

Gwen gasped. "I couldn't!"

"Don't forget that she believes you're my special lady friend."

"Surely you're not intending to prolong that charade." Gwen was shocked and couldn't help showing it.

"Actually, it sort of backfired on me," Zane admitted. "I didn't think ahead to what could happen if my family liked you." *Or if I liked you.* Gwen stirred him in unique ways. She was pretty and sexy, and he never would forget how she'd looked in that wet T-shirt. If only she would invite him into her house so they could talk in private. He really felt that they were on display for the whole neighborhood to see while they talked in her driveway.

"A rather crucial oversight, don't you think?" Gwen said dryly.

"A damn stupid oversight is more like it. Anyhow, I seem to be up the creek without a paddle. Would you go to Vanessa and Devin's with me on Wednesday?''

Frowning, Gwen paced a small circle. Then she stopped and shook her head. "I'm sorry, but I have to say no. I told you I don't date, and you really should have believed me because it's the truth. And I agreed to the charade as a one-time deal only. I'm sure you can come up with some kind of story for your sister about you and me not seeing each other anymore."

Zane cleared his throat. "I probably can. Gwen, my throat feels dry as dust. Could I have a drink of water?" Thinking fast, realizing that she could go into the house and bring a glass of water out to him, he added, "And also use your bathroom?"

Gwen hesitated. Compared to his home, hers was a hovel. And it was never completely clean and picked up. She simply did not have the time to keep an immaculate house. Were there even clean towels in the bathroom? She couldn't remember.

But how could she refuse Zane a drink of water and the use of her bathroom? "All right," she agreed, albeit uneasily. "I'll get my key ring from the van."

While Gwen strode to her van, Zane realized that talking her into going to Vanessa's dinner party would be a mistake. He wanted to know Gwen better, and at this early stage of what he honestly wanted to be a budding relationship, he shouldn't be pressuring her into more socializing with his family. He should be furthering his own interests—and, hopefully, hers—by convincing her to change her attitude toward dating. In truth, he had never known a young, beautiful woman who didn't date at all, and he couldn't understand why Gwen would live that way.

She returned with her key ring and walked past him

to her front door. He followed, she unlocked the door and they both went in. There was no foyer, Zane noticed. The front door opened directly into a small living room that contained a sofa, two chairs, a couple of end tables with lamps and a television set. There was not enough space in the room for anything else, and he realized that Gwen's living room wasn't as big as his personal closet. He also saw evidence of her children scattered around—some stuffed animals, a doll and some tiny toy cars.

"The bathroom is down that hall," Gwen said. She spoke rather stiffly, because she'd seen Zane looking around. If he was shocked by her plain little house and mismatched furniture, he had better not say so, she thought with a prideful squaring of her shoulders. She herself might wish for a larger, nicer house and all that went with it, but this was the best she could afford, and Zane Fortune could like it or lump it. She would never apologize for having so little, especially to him, a man who had everything.

"Thanks." Zane sauntered down the hall.

Gwen's hands weren't quite steady as she prepared two glasses of ice water in her minuscule kitchen. Having Zane in her house was unnerving, and she actually prayed that she had picked up all the damp towels in her one and only bathroom, and had set out clean towels that morning.

She thought of the kids' bath toys in the tub and the shower curtain that she'd been intending to replace, the threadbare bath mat draped over the edge of the tub and the worn little rag rug that was always askew in front of the sink. She sighed heavily, almost despondently. Zane Fortune was definitely getting a firsthand look at how the other half lived.

But she was letting his presence in her home get her down, and she didn't like that underdog feeling one little bit. She was staring out the window over the kitchen sink wondering why some people were so lucky with money and others struggled all their lives to scrape by when she felt Zane's hands on each side of her waist. Obviously she'd been so deep in thought that she hadn't heard him come up behind her. Either that or he had deliberately snuck up.

She closed her eyes and savored the moment. He exuded the cleanest, most marvelous scent, and if it wasn't such a foolish fantasy, she would have liked to stand there for the rest of the day and just breathe.

But he had a lot more in mind than mere breathing, she realized when she felt his mouth nuzzling the side of her neck.

Slipping away from both his hands and mouth, she turned and faced him. "Is that the real reason you wanted to come in?" she asked, and was startled by the breathless quality she heard in her own voice. Something inside her groaned. Why did he have to be the most gorgeous human being on the face of the earth?

But gorgeous or not, she didn't trust him. And if rumors about his reputation were accurate, she *shouldn't* trust him. He was not the kind of man she should even be friends with, because reputations were somewhat contagious, and she certainly didn't want his rubbing off on her. She wouldn't want people thinking of her as one more of Zane Fortune's conquests.

She gave him a troubled look, just as he said, "I asked to come in because I wasn't comfortable talking in your driveway. That's the truth, Gwen."

"Is it?" she asked quietly, though her expression remained distraught.

"I'm not saying I don't find you enormously attractive," Zane said, also speaking in a quiet tone. "I do, Gwen. You're a very beautiful, desirable woman."

"Especially when I'm dressed in worn-out jeans and an old shirt," she said sarcastically.

"Surely you don't believe that clothes mean that much. You couldn't be anything but beautiful, whatever you happened to be wearing."

She threw up her hands. "For God's sake, Zane, I wasn't born yesterday! If clothes didn't make a difference, you'd be buying yours off the rack, not having them custom made. So please don't insult my intelligence by telling me that my beauty and desirability are knocking you out. I know exactly how I look today, and it sure isn't beautiful!"

Zane leaned one hip against a counter, folded his arms across his chest and stared at her. "You really don't know how to take a compliment, do you?"

"Since I haven't heard a genuine compliment in a very long time, I wouldn't know." She could tell that he was all set to give her an argument, and she took a hurried, impatient breath. "I have to deliver that table before five. Are you ready to leave now?"

"Will you go to Vanessa's with me on Wednesday?"

"No."

"And there's nothing I could do or say to change your mind?"

Gwen was scared that he was on the verge of offering her money again. She hoped he wouldn't. She hoped it so much that her fingernails dug into her palms as she clenched her hands into fists.

"I hope you won't even try," she said with a slight quake in her voice.

He studied her for a few long moments, then pushed himself away from the counter. "Okay, you win. I won't ask you out again. But you don't win every point," he added, and took the three steps between them, clasped her by her upper arms and pulled her forward so that his face was but a breath from hers. "This point is mine," he whispered just before covering her lips with his.

He kissed her until her knees got wobbly…until she was digging her fingers into the front of his shirt….until her body was burning and yearning….until her mind was so dazed she'd lost track of her own name.

And then he *stopped* kissing her. While she grabbed for the back of a chair to steady herself, he said huskily, "That was a pretty good point, wasn't it? I do have to ask myself, though, which one of us got the most benefit from it. I'll be going now. Maybe we'll run into each other again sometime when you're at my house, cleaning something, or bathing Alamo. So long, darlin'. See you around."

Gwen moved around the chair on shaky legs and all but fell onto it. Had she ever been so thoroughly kissed before? she wondered as her mind spun dizzily.

Six

Gwen was badly shaken. Responding to Zane Fortune was a fool's game. During her entire adult life she had made love with one man—her children's father—and the voracious manner in which she had kissed Zane back seemed like an insult to her deceased husband's memory.

After walking the floor and literally wringing her hands for a good half hour, however, Gwen's perspective on that kiss began to change. First of all, her kissing any man as a widow had nothing at all to do with Paul. She'd been a good and faithful wife and had no guilt or regrets where Paul and her marriage were concerned. Besides, there was nothing wrong, sinful or criminal about a kiss between two consenting adults. In fact, Gwen finally concluded unhappily, the one and only problem with that kiss was that Zane Fortune had administered it and that she had liked it far too much. In truth, she had liked it so much that if Zane had not put on the brakes, they very well might be in her bed right now!

That idea scared her to death. The last thing she needed in her problem-laden life was a too rich, too good-looking, too worldly-wise bachelor who could never understand her, her kids or her life-style. In fact, she should have slapped Zane Fortune's face today, she thought indignantly. What made him think he had the right to kiss her anytime he felt like it? That was twice now, and he'd just better not try it a third time!

Gwen's lethargy since Zane's departure suddenly vanished, and she hurried out to the garage for the little table that needed delivery. Carrying it to her van, she saw the dents and scratches, which reminded her of the accident, and her heart sank. Instead of paying bills or putting something away for a rainy day with that two thousand, she was going to have to pay for the repairs to Zane's car. Why hadn't he stayed on his own side of town today?

Muttering, Gwen got behind the steering wheel of the van and drove to Marion Kravitz's home. The woman was delighted with the table and would have chatted about it for an hour if Gwen hadn't told her that she had another appointment. She collected $180 for the table and left, sorry about lying to a woman as nice as Mrs. Kravitz, but forgiving herself for the lie because she simply could not bear idle chitchat with so much on her mind.

Driving away from the Kravitz home, Gwen heaved a ponderous sigh. It never failed to happen, she thought despondently. If she somehow managed to earn a few extra dollars, something occurred to make her spend them. Damn Zane for parking in her driveway today! And for even thinking she might go to his sister's house for dinner when she'd told him in plain English that she didn't date.

Did he finally have the message now, or was he going to come up with another excuse to badger her? Of course there was no avoiding some sort of contact about the repairs to his car.

Gwen groaned. Nothing ever worked in her favor—absolutely nothing. One thing she'd been planning to do with that two thousand was reinstate her auto insurance. What incredible irony.

Phoning Vanessa could not be avoided, although Zane didn't place the call until late that night because of the hours he'd spent searching for a believable reason why he and Gwen would not be having dinner with his sister and her husband. Ordinarily, telling Vanessa, or any other member of his family, that he was no longer seeing a particular woman wouldn't bother him in the least. Yet the thought of saying it about Gwen didn't just bother him, it chafed at raw nerves.

A dozen times he asked himself why he had kissed her again. Had he hoped to accomplish something with Gwen, or had he simply lost control of his normal good sense for a few minutes today? The fact that she'd kissed back was like a melody repeating in his mind—ever-present, haunting, frustrating.

Shaking his head to dispel the memory of the kiss, he braced himself to call Vanessa and explain that he and Gwen were no longer seeing each other. That would officially end this charade once and for all.

But somehow he just couldn't do it. When he finally dialed Vanessa's number, he told her that Gwen had other plans for dinner on Wednesday.

"Oh, that's too bad," Vanessa said, sounding disappointed. "How about Thursday night? Or Friday?"

Obviously Vanessa wasn't giving up. Zane's expression became grim, because now he was going to have to expand his lie.

"She's busy all week, Vanessa. Sorry."

"All week? Goodness, I didn't realize she was that busy. Does that mean you won't be seeing her at all this week?"

"Uh, just in brief spurts."

"Well, that must put an awful strain on your relationship. Is Gwen tied up for social or business reasons?"

"Hmm…mostly business," Zane said after taking a second to think.

"I do recall her saying something about owning and operating her own business."

"Yes, she does, and I guess at times the, uh, paperwork gets a bit overwhelming."

"Surely she has clerical help, Zane."

Zane was tired of fabricating stories about Gwen. "Vanessa, I have another call coming in. Sorry to cut our conversation short, but I had better take it."

"Yes, it could be Gwen," Vanessa agreed with a teasing lilt in her voice. "Good night, Zane. Oh, let me know when you and Gwen do have a free evening. I still want the chance to get to know her better."

The strangest weakness washed over Zane as he said good-night and hung up the phone. He wished to high heaven that he'd never brought Gwen to that wedding. Not only couldn't Vanessa forget her, neither could he!

Gwen had picked up her kids at the usual time that day, but she didn't get a chance to really talk to Ramona until nine, after the kids were in bed and she herself was showered and wearing her nightclothes.

"This is becoming a habit," Gwen said after dialing Ramona's number and hearing her normal brisk hello.

"What is?" Ramona asked.

"Calling you after the kids are down for the night."

"Well, it's a good habit. We certainly don't get much opportunity to talk when you bring the kids over in the morning or pick them up in the evening. So tell me what's new in your life.''

''Probably the news flash of the day is that I ran into Zane Fortune's car with my van,'' Gwen said dryly.

''You *what?* Good Lord, Gwen, what happened?''

''He was parked in my driveway, and I didn't see his car until it was too late.''

''That damn hedge.''

''Yes, that damn hedge,'' Gwen agreed. ''But it isn't like I was making that turn for the first time, Ramona. Do you remember last summer when I almost plowed into my dad's car for the same reason? That was a near miss instead of a crash only because my mind was on driving instead of fifty other things. Today I wasn't that lucky. Neither Zane nor I were hurt, thank God, but his car was. And guess what? I had to let my auto insurance lapse last month.''

''Oh, Gwen,'' Ramona groaned. ''Why didn't you borrow the cost of the premium from me? Or from your folks? You can't be driving around without insurance.''

''I will not ask my folks for another penny, and if I started borrowing money from you, we probably wouldn't be friends for long. Forget that idea. I will never borrow from you, and that's that. Can you believe how ironic life can be at times? Zane paid me two-thousand dollars, which I deposited in my checking account this morning. One of the things I was going to do with that money was reinstate my car insurance. Before I got it done, though, I ran into his car.''

''It's the pits,'' Ramona said gloomily. ''I suppose he was all bent and upset over the accident.''

"Actually, he was nice about it," Gwen said slowly, realizing it was true.

"That was big of him, but why was he parked in your driveway in the first place?"

"Ramona, I really don't understand Zane Fortune. For some reason he wants to keep his family believing that he and I are a hot item. One of his sisters asked him to bring me to dinner at her house, and he came by to ask if I'd go."

"Well?"

"Well, what?"

"Gwen, what did you say to his dinner invitation?" Ramona sounded a trifle impatient.

"I said no, what else would I say? And after he kissed me, I was darn glad—"

"Whoa, there. He *kissed* you?"

"Yes, he did, and I should have slapped his face. I'm furious with myself because I didn't. He's much too bold, Ramona, and I'm sure he thinks he can do anything he wants just because he's a Fortune."

"Gwen, where did he kiss you?"

"On the mouth."

"No, no, I meant *where?* In your driveway?"

"Uh, no, we were in the house by then."

"You invited him in?"

"Only because he asked to use the bathroom. I could hardly say no to that." Ramona fell silent, until Gwen said, "Ramona? Are you still there?"

"Gwen, have you considered the possibility of Zane Fortune genuinely liking you?"

"Oh, really, Ramona," Gwen said with a derogatory sniff. "If Zane wants anything at all from me beyond my help in deluding his family, it could only be one thing. And I am not going to have an affair with any man, especially not with a man who's had everything his way since the day he was born.''

''And that's how you see Zane? How you feel about him?''

''You'd feel the same way if you met him. He's just too...perfect.''

''Oh, I can see why you wouldn't want him,'' Ramona said with a small laugh. ''I mean, what woman would want a 'perfect' man?''

''I didn't say his character was perfect—his reputation with women would make a soap opera.''

''So what's perfect about him, then?''

''His...his looks, I guess,'' Gwen stammered. She laughed awkwardly. ''Can you believe that I'm finding this conversation embarrassing? You and I have been able to talk about anything for a long time, and now because a man kissed me I'm all red-faced and tongue-tied. Silly, isn't it?''

''It might not be silly at all,'' Ramona said gently. ''But let's talk about something else and let you off the hook for now.''

They talked for another hour about other things. But when Gwen finally went to bed, she lay there for a long time and thought that Ramona could possibly be right: Her feelings for Zane might not be silly at all. They could be...serious!

''No,'' she whispered as panic rose in her throat. ''No, no, no!'' How could she label feelings that even she didn't fully comprehend as either silly *or* serious? She had to stop trying to figure herself out where Zane was concerned, she thought a bit frantically. She hadn't suddenly turned into someone else, after all. She was just plain Gwen Hutton, and Zane Fortune was miles above her in looks, money and position.

She'd be wise to keep that one crucial fact firmly fixed in her mind.

By the following Friday, Gwen was uneasily wondering why she'd heard nothing from Zane about the repairs to his car. She returned library books for elderly Harry Adkins, shopped for a birthday gift for Tom Cunningham's secretary, bathed two cats and a dog for Elizabeth Rondell, and literally ran from job to job all day—only taking one unscheduled break when she drove past a garage sale and stopped to check the merchandise. All the while Gwen kept thinking it was peculiar that Zane hadn't contacted her about the repairs to his car.

Three times she dashed home to check the messages on her machines. She knew there were much better models on the market—ones that would allow her to retrieve her messages by phone—and that hers were very outdated, but they were just one more example of how she had to make do with things she already owned. Buying anything new, was always a major undertaking. Gwen had become very adept at mending and making clothes last, but there was nothing she could do about shoes, which one child or another constantly seemed to be outgrowing.

On her third trip home, Gwen listened to a few messages—none from Zane—and decided to get to the bottom of his silence. She needed to know the exact cost of his car repairs so she could feel free to use the rest of that two-thousand—if there was any left over—for other things. Actually, it was darn inconsiderate of him not to have immediately phoned her with that information, she thought while dialing the Fortune company number.

"Zane Fortune's office. Heather Moore speaking," his secretary said.

"Heather, this is Gwen Hutton. Is Mr. Fortune in?"

"Why...yes," Heather said slowly, obviously surprised by Gwen's question.

Gwen understood Heather's reaction. Heather was the person who had hired her for specified jobs at Zane's home, the person Gwen had always talked to about anything concerning those jobs, and now here she was asking if Mr. Fortune was in. Gwen suspected that her question had confused Heather, but if Zane hadn't told his secretary that Gwen had run into his elegant car with her old van, she certainly wasn't going to do it.

Instead she said, "May I speak to him, Heather?" Gwen was proud of the calmness of her voice, because she didn't feel at all calm. In fact, she was downright nervous about calling Zane. She knew that she would never phone him—or any other client— for a frivolous reason, but he did owe her an answer on the cost of those repairs, and that was by no means frivolous to her.

"I'm going to put you on hold for a moment while I check with Mr. Fortune and find out if he's free to take your call," Heather said.

Music immediately began playing in Gwen's ear, and she realized how easily Zane could avoid talking to her. As polite as Heather Moore always was on the phone, she was first and foremost the consummate secretary, loyal to and protective of her boss.

"Gwen?"

Her heart nearly stopped when she heard Zane's voice in her ear. "Yes...hello," she stammered.

"This is a pleasant surprise," he said, sounding as

though he really meant it, which instantly put Gwen on guard.

"I'm sorry to bother you at work, but I really need to know how much the repairs to your car are going to cost. Have you found out yet?"

"Uh, no. I haven't had the time to take the car to a body shop. Maybe I'll be able to get to it next week."

"I can't believe you're driving a car with a caved-in trunk."

"It's not that bad, Gwen. The trunk has some dents, but it's not caved in. Besides, I'm not driving it. I have more than one car."

"Of course, how silly of me," she drawled. "I should have thought of that."

"You sound angry."

"I'm not angry, just a little impatient. Do you have even a ballpark figure for the cost of the repairs?"

He knew to the penny. The car was already repaired and parked downstairs in the company garage. He was driving a sports utility vehicle, which he'd recently purchased, and having fun with it. But he knew if he told Gwen the truth, she'd have a fit because he'd dared to insult her integrity and independence.

"I really know nothing about auto body repairs, Gwen," he said. That, at least, was true. "My estimate would be worse than none." That was partially true.

"I thought men knew about these things," Gwen said irritably.

"Probably a lot of them do. I just don't happen to be one of them. Gwen, I know I said I wouldn't ask you out again, but how about a movie tonight? Dinner too, if you'd like."

Gwen found herself unable to say an immediate and

irrevocable no. A movie date sounded so darn great. She wouldn't have to pretend to be someone other than herself because none of Zane's family would be around. A good movie, theater popcorn and a handsome escort. In her estimation that combination was pretty much the perfect date.

"How about it?" Zane persisted.

"I...I'd have to say no to dinner, because after being away from my kids all day, I need to see them and they need to see me. But once they're in bed..." Gwen bit her lip. She would have to find a baby-sitter in her own neighborhood, someone to come to the house and stay with the kids for a couple of hours. Ramona would gladly watch the kids, but only at her own house.

Gwen's stomach churned. She shouldn't be doing this. She should repeat to Zane once again that she didn't date, and say it firmly, maybe even harshly, so that he would never ask her out again.

Instead she heard herself saying, "I might be able to make the nine o'clock feature. If I can find a baby-sitter, that is."

"Well, darlin', just get your pretty self in gear and find that sitter. I'll pick you up at eight. See you then."

He hung up! Gwen stared at the dead phone in her hand as though it just might decide to bite her. Then she hung up.

For the rest of the day she worried about having agreed to that movie date, and she didn't tell Ramona about it when she picked up her kids. While driving home Gwen wondered if she was ashamed or guilty or something else entirely. She had to be feeling something odd, or she would have mentioned the date to her best friend.

The kids were safely buckled into their seat belts, but their noise finally penetrated Gwen's concentration. Donnie, she realized, was teasing Ashley and making her scream. Tiny Mindy added to the din by screaming whenever Ashley did, just because she mimicked almost everything her big sister did.

"Hey, you guys, knock it off!" Gwen shouted. She didn't like to shout at her children, but sometimes it was the only way to be heard. "Donnie, stop teasing your sisters."

They quieted down, and Gwen heaved a sigh. What on earth would a man like Zane Fortune do around three noisy little kids?

A voice in her head answered: *He'd probably go nuts in five minutes flat.*

When they got home, Gwen again prepared her kids' favorite food for supper—macaroni-and-cheese and hot dogs. They ate, then she let them play while she cleaned up the kitchen and hurried herself through a shower and shampoo. Next came the children's baths, a lot of horseplay while Gwen got them into their pajamas, and finally the tucking-in process—a bedtime story, prayers and a whole bunch of hugs and kisses. This was Gwen's most emotional time of day, the precious moments when she could shower her kids with love and they weren't bouncing up and down too much to notice.

But time flew by and it was ten minutes to eight when the baby-sitter, Norma Blake—an older woman who supplemented her social security checks with neighborhood baby-sitting jobs—knocked on Gwen's front door. A harried Gwen let her in, told her the kids were in bed and to make herself at home, then dashed to her bedroom to get dressed. She had no time to pick and choose, and she grabbed a floral print skirt and a white sweater from her closet. Shedding the robe she'd been wearing since her shower, she dressed at the speed of light and then ran for the bathroom to put on a little makeup and do something with her hair.

At five minutes after eight, Gwen heard the doorbell. Her heart started pounding nervously, and she felt a little bit sick to her stomach. Looking in the mirror she saw the almost stricken look on her face. What on earth had prompted her to accept Zane's movie invitation? She knew she shouldn't get involved with him. Yet somehow she seemed to be a pawn in something much bigger than herself. She felt swept along by events beyond her control.

Detouring to her bedroom for her purse, she bravely lifted her chin and then headed down the hall toward her living room. Just before reaching it, she heard Zane conversing with Mrs. Blake. He sounded mellow and relaxed, and he was asking about Mrs. Blake's grown children.

Gwen halted her stride and listened. It was clear Zane was charming the woman, but why was he drawing her out about her children when he hadn't asked Gwen one question about *her* kids? *Because it's a safe topic with an elderly woman, and it wouldn't be with you!*

He didn't even know how many children she had, nor did he seem to care. Resentment made Gwen go stiff. Beneath all of his fine, polished manners, he was a self-absorbed jerk. She and her kids were a package deal, didn't he realize that? No man would get anywhere with her if he excluded her kids. Since Zane seemed focused on her alone, he must not be thinking long term. A quickie affair was all he would ever give her, or any other woman in her situation.

Gwen's heart was suddenly pounding nervously. She should not be spending any more time with Zane Fortune, not even for something so innocent as a movie date. Her mind began racing, searching for a tactful way to get out of this evening, but she couldn't think of an excuse that would sound sensible to Zane, or even to herself, for that matter.

Other than resorting to outright rudeness, she was stuck. She'd made a dire mistake by saying yes to this date, and now she would have to live with it.

Okay, fine, she thought resentfully. She'd go to the movie with him. But if he wanted her to even speak to him again, he had better ask a few questions about her kids tonight.

After taking a deep breath, Gwen pasted on a smile and walked into the living room.

Seven

Gwen was initially unnerved by the mere handful of people in the theater. Everyone was sitting so far from each other that it was almost as though she and Zane were alone. He'd taken her to a cinema complex with twelve theaters, and the movie they'd chosen to see wasn't crowded. Then, Zane had led her to seats at the back of the theater, which added to Gwen's sense of isolation.

For a while, once the movie began and she became interested in it, that feeling diminished. But then, about halfway through the picture, she set her empty popcorn and soft drink containers on the floor, as did Zane. A warning bell went off in her head when he laid his arm along the top of her seat back.

"Don't do that," she whispered.

His response was to put his mouth close to her ear and whisper, "You smell as sweet as honeysuckle."

A chill that was pure thrill went up her spine. His breath on her ear and his nearness were causing some intense physical reactions.

But she couldn't let that happen, and she whispered, "If you don't intend to watch the movie, then I would just as soon leave."

"If we leave, will you come to my house?"

She turned her head to glare at him. "Don't be absurd!" She realized instantly that she should not have faced him, because then his mouth was only an inch from hers. Even sitting down, her knees felt weak. In fact, she was feeling rather weak all over. Like it or not, Zane affected her—the first man who had touched her emotions at all since she was widowed.

He kissed her. She'd known he was going to the second she'd turned her head. And she allowed it— encouraged it, in fact.

It was a slow-burning, undemanding kiss. His mouth moved lazily on hers, and she did nothing to stop it. Rather, she let her head fall back to his arm and parted her lips for his tongue. Her vow to singe his gall with righteous indignation if he tried to kiss her a third time seemed very far away, and even though it vaguely passed through her mind, she was too lost in the kiss itself to really think of anything else.

In truth, it was lovely to be kissed in that dark little theater by such a handsome, vital man, and she could not prevent herself from responding. Zane smelled heavenly. She *felt* heavenly, and dreamy and completely out of touch with reality.

"Gwen...my beautiful Gwen," he whispered huskily before kissing her again.

While his lips moved on hers, his endearment gradually sank in. But she couldn't deny the sexual excitement rising within her, and she again responded.

His left arm was still behind her head, and she felt his right hand move to her waist. That's all right, she thought dizzily. A few kisses really didn't mean that much, and his hand on her waist certainly wasn't too far out of line. She seemed to have completely lost sight of every misgiving she'd had about Zane. Her heart was beating madly and the sensual weakness in her system was so delicious that she uttered no objections whatsoever.

Zane was so elated over her response that his head was spinning. He wished they were alone somewhere, but in a quick glance around he saw that the few other patrons were engrossed in the film and were all sitting more to the center of the theater. Even if someone did happen to look their way, they would see very little.

He was wary of suggesting anything that might destroy Gwen's mood, such as again asking her to go to his house. So he accepted what he had—her soft, luscious lips and her unexpected participation.

But he really did want so much more. He ached from wanting more, and he wondered if she knew how potently she affected him. It wasn't something a man asked a woman, though, so he suffered that particular discomfort in silence, even while realizing that it was only going to get worse if he kept on kissing her. And then, almost absentmindedly, he dropped his hand from her waist to her thigh.

Gwen was so absorbed in the way he kissed that she barely noticed his hand shifting. But a few moments later, when his hand was under the voluminous folds of her skirt and caressing her bare thigh on a path to her panties, she gasped.

Tearing her mouth from his, she whispered, "No, Zane."

"Let me touch you," he pleaded in her ear. "I want you so much. Let me pleasure you." Without waiting for permission, he pushed aside the band of her panties between her legs and began stroking her most sensitive spot.

Her emotions went wild. Moaning quietly, she

turned her face into the front of his shirt. "Open your legs a little more," he whispered.

She shocked herself by doing as he asked—nothing had ever felt so good as his hand between her legs. At least it hadn't in a very long time. She sat there and let him touch and stroke and caress until she nearly shouted from a climax so powerful it brought tears to her eyes.

He kissed the top of her head and whispered, "You are wonderful."

Wonderful? Mortified is more like it. More embarrassed than she could ever before remember being, she disentangled herself from him, unsteadily got to her feet and headed for the aisle, kicking over the popcorn and soft drink containers as she went.

Zane stared after her for a moment as though struck, then jumped up, grabbed his jacket and followed. She stayed a good twenty feet ahead of him until they were outdoors, but then he caught up with her.

"Gwen, stop running," he said as he clasped his hand around her arm. She faced him, and he saw the tears in her eyes. "You're crying. Honey, what's wrong?" he asked gently.

She wiped away tears and looked everywhere but into his eyes. "I'm sure you know."

He was stunned by the embittered defeat he heard in her voice. "No, I don't know."

His answer angered her. "You…you humiliated me!"

"Making love humiliates you? Gwen, there's something terribly wrong with that attitude."

"It's your attitude that needs some examination and revision," she snapped. "We were in a public place, for God's sake, and you…you…" Embarrassment seared her again and she couldn't find the words to say what he'd done to her.

"Gwen, is that what's bothering you? You think someone saw what we were doing? They didn't. It was dark and no one was sitting within twenty feet of us. The few people in there were watching the movie, and no one was paying the slightest attention to us."

She was finally getting her wits about her, and she was angry, fiercely angry. And hurt. They weren't lovers, they were just barely friends, and he'd taken advantage of her. That sort of behavior might be normal for him, but it wasn't normal for her.

Even so, her mind was clearing enough to see both sides of the situation. If she hadn't gone out with him, he wouldn't have had the chance to take advantage of her. To be perfectly and painfully honest, tonight's embarrassing fiasco was really her own fault. Zane's reputation with women was common knowledge around San Antonio, after all.

She suddenly felt bogged down with self-accusations and incriminations. *You let him kiss you. In fact, you kissed him back. That's three times now that you kissed him back. Why wouldn't he think he could go farther in that dark theater? You've been easy with him.*

At long last she looked directly into his eyes, forcing her gaze to remain steady and hard. "What took place between us tonight, or anything even remotely similar, is not going to happen again," she said coldly. "I know you're considered to be a smooth operator with the ladies, and I guess you proved it in the theater with me, but this is the end of the line, Zane. I will never see you socially again. If you wish to cancel your working relationship with Help-Mate, that's fine too. I still need the figures on your car repairs, but I would appreciate your having Heather call me with that information when you finally get it.''

To her astonishment, Zane laughed. ''Aren't you getting a bit carried away? All I did was—''

She broke in before he could get explicit. ''Think what you want. I'm going home. In a *taxi*,'' she added as she started walking quickly down the street.

Zane ran to catch up. ''Gwen, don't you think this is getting a little ridiculous? My car is right over there.''

She shot him a dirty look and kept walking. The cinema complex was part of a large mall, and most of the establishments were closed for the day. Hailing a cab was probably out of the question, but she could call one from a pay phone. There *must* be pay phones somewhere nearby.

Much to her surprise and relief, she spotted a taxi cruising the mall's parking lot. She took off after it, shouting, ''Taxi!''

Zane stopped in his tracks, stunned. What was wrong with the woman? He certainly hadn't forced himself on her in the theater. Why had she let him get so familiar if she hadn't wanted it? He thinned his lips. She'd wanted exactly what he'd done, dammit, and how dare she resent him for it now?

Grimly he watched while the cab stopped and she got into it. Then he strode to his car, climbed in and headed for home.

Maria Cassidy knew that she'd taken a big risk by attending Parker and Hannah's wedding, all because of her meddling brother, Cole. Maria's closest neighbor in the seedy trailer park in which she had previ-

ously lived had been eager to tell her about the nosy
man who'd shown up one day when she wasn't home,
walking all around her trailer, looking in every window. The gossipy woman had told her the man said
he was her brother.

Maria had nearly hyperventilated from fear. Cole
could not have missed seeing Bryan's crib, playpen
and high chair. Anyone with half a brain would know
a baby or small child was living with her. Even though
she hoped Cole had assumed that she was merely
baby-sitting someone else's child, Maria's confidence
had slipped badly.

She'd told herself that Cole couldn't possibly know
the child was Bryan, Matthew Fortune's kidnapped
son. He certainly couldn't know anything about her
plan to take down the Fortunes. How she'd plotted to
have her own Fortune baby by getting impregnated at
a sperm bank with a donation Matthew had made
years ago. How she'd brought that baby—a Fortune
heir!—to Bryan's christening party and he'd been mis-
taken as Bryan and kidnapped. With her son gone,
she'd had no choice but to take Bryan herself.

But her fear had overwhelmed rationality, and she
had thrown her belongings into her old car, taking
Bryan and making a hasty getaway.

She'd driven around frantically for hours on back
roads trying to figure out what to do next. When night
fell, she checked into an inexpensive motel. Money
was always a problem, and now she couldn't even go
to work because she dare not chance leaving Bryan
with anyone else.

She had paced the floor for most of that first night,
hating Cole for not minding his own business, hating
the Fortunes for never having to worry about money,

despising her mother for believing that Ryan Fortune was going to marry her—all in all pretty much hating everything and everyone. Dark feelings had swirled within Maria that night, and she'd muttered out loud while she walked the worn carpet in that pathetic little room.

"Now what're you gonna do? Your money will last about a week, then what? Maybe you should just drive off and leave Bryan here. Someone will find him in the morning."

She'd mumbled about that idea for about an hour, then started thinking of the ransom money she could get for the boy. When she'd sent a ransom note five months ago, she'd been too nervous of getting caught to pick the ransom up. But this could be her one and only chance to get rich. Maybe she should try again.

Just before dawn she'd remembered going to her mealy-mouthed sister Hannah's wedding. She hadn't intended to go to the affair, but it had seemed like a propitious opportunity to borrow some money from her mother.

She knew if Cole had told anyone about seeing baby furniture in her trailer, and someone was smart enough to add two and two, showing herself at *any* affair could be dangerous business. But so would simply phoning her mother at the Double Crown Ranch and asking for a loan. She had figured that at least at the wedding, Lily would be too busy to grill her, and maybe Cole wouldn't even be there.

Now, thinking back, Maria knew that Cole had been surprised to see her at the wedding, but she'd cleverly avoided him all night. And she'd stayed on the sidelines of the merry gathering until she'd spotted an opportunity to talk to her mother alone. It had been easy to borrow five-hundred dollars, because Lily had such a soft heart when it came to her children.

But even five hundred wouldn't last long. If she was going to ask again for ransom for Bryan, she had to figure out a foolproof way to go about it. It was frustrating to realize that all she knew of such things had been picked up from movies and novels. The real thing seemed vastly different from fiction and also treacherously laden with pitfalls. The thought of being caught and going to prison was horrifying.

And so Maria sat in that little motel room for days and days, one minute dreaming of fabulous wealth, the next sinking into deep despair. Her emotions were becoming more unstable by the hour. She was getting dangerously close to the breaking point.

During the taxi ride to her house, Gwen realized how deeply troubled she really was, how shaken. She stared out the side window of the cab and saw none of the passing city. Never in her life had she been part of the sort of intimacy that had taken place in the theater, and she could hardly believe she had let Zane go so far.

But there was no way she could gloss over the facts and pretend that she hadn't reveled in the most sensual thing a man had ever done to her. In a public place, no less. How could she have let it happen? What kind of woman had she become since meeting Zane? While it would be easy to put all the blame on him, she knew in her soul that she was far from blameless.

Before she got home, her mood turned sad and melancholy. She could not see Zane again, not in any capacity. He was a dangerous man for a woman like her to be fooling around with. It would probably be best if she broke all ties with him by phoning Heather and telling her that Help-Mate was cutting back on clients, or some such story. Any lie would do, as long as it completely eliminated further contact with Zane.

Tears began seeping down her cheeks, and she angrily dashed them away. Dammit, she was not going to cry over Zane Fortune, she wasn't! Surely she wasn't that big a fool.

At her house she paid the cab driver and went inside. Mrs. Blake looked surprised. "You're home early."

Gwen dug into her purse for money. "A little," she murmured.

"Your mother called," Mrs. Blake said as she accepted her pay.

"Did she want me to call her back when I got home?"

"No, she said she would phone again tomorrow." Mrs. Blake smiled. "She seemed very pleased to hear you had a date."

Gwen's heart sank. "She didn't happen to ask who I went out with, did she?"

"As a matter of fact, she did."

"And you told her?"

Mrs. Blake instantly looked worried. "Shouldn't I have? Oh, Gwen, I'm sorry if I spoke out of turn."

"It's all right," Gwen said to reassure the older woman, even though she wished with all her heart that Zane's name had not come up. Her parents were wonderful people, but they had been extremely protective of her and their grandchildren since Paul's death. They were not apt to approve of her dating a man with Zane's reputation.

Sighing, she walked the woman to the front door

and let her out. "Good night, Mrs. Blake. Thanks for baby-sitting."

"Just let me know if you ever need me again, Gwen."

"Thank you, I will."

After Mrs. Blake had gone, Gwen turned out all the lights and sat in her dark living room. She knew that she should never think of that incident in the theater again, never recall how warm and womanly Zane had made her feel. Regardless of her sensual urges, she and Zane didn't match, they were not a fit. And not once had he referred to her kids, not by question, not by innuendo, not by so much as a hint that he even recognized she had children.

Bitterness rose in her throat. He was a self-centered jerk, and if her heart was just a little bit broken because of Zane Fortune, she had no one to blame but herself.

Eight

"Zane? Lily here. We're having a family barbecue on Saturday, hoping, of course, that it's not too short notice and everyone will come. How are you set for Saturday?"

"You're planning on strictly family, Lily?"

Lily laughed. "That was my original plan, but your father has already invited a few friends, so I suppose I should stop calling it a family barbecue. It will be mostly family...I think. You know how these things can grow. Oh, by the way, we would love to see Gwen again, so please bring her with you. If you can make it yourself, of course."

I'd love to see Gwen again too, but that doesn't look very promising. Frowning, Zane leaned back in his chair, put his feet up on a corner of his desk and, without really seeing, stared out a window of his office while he took a second to mull over the invitation.

Of all the social activities that took place on the ranch, he liked the barbecues best. Everyone brought their kids and wore jeans and boots, the food was always terrific, and horses were provided for anyone wanting to take a ride. Yes, this was one affair he would love to attend.

"Lily, I can't speak for Gwen at the moment, but count me in," he said.

"Wonderful. Zane, you know I'm not ordinarily a

nosy person, but I am curious about Gwen. Let me bring my inquisitiveness down to one question. Are you planning to ask her to come with you?''

''Uh, let's just say that I'd like her to go but there are no guarantees.''

''Fair enough. I'll count you as two, just in case you bring Gwen or someone else.''

''Thanks, Lily. See you on Saturday.''

''Yes, on Saturday. And pray this incredible weather holds,'' Lily said. '''Bye for now.''

Zane hung up and continued to stare out the window as he wondered how best to approach Gwen. Since their movie date, he hadn't tried to contact her, but she was just about all he could think of. He could not remember ever wanting a woman more, and while he wasn't sure that he liked being so strung out over one particular woman, there didn't seem to be anything he could do about it. She was in his blood; it was as simple as that.

But what bothered him so much was that his feelings for Gwen were not simple at all. He certainly knew women who were more beautiful. And women who would do almost anything to spend time with him; sex had never been a scarce commodity. But lately Gwen was the only woman who turned him on. It was damn disturbing.

His most constant and perturbing thought was of his hand between her legs in the theater. She'd been so hot and wet, and whenever he thought of those intensely sexual minutes he wanted to make love to her so badly that he physically ached.

He knew he wasn't his normal self at all, and that his work was suffering right along with his body. But he couldn't keep his mind in the office, where it belonged, for even eight hours a day. It was with Gwen, even though he could only imagine where she might be or what she might be doing.

He wished he could get back to where he'd been before meeting her. In his soul, though, he knew it wasn't going to happen. But why in heaven's name was he pursuing a woman with her inhibitions, her seemingly endless problems, her peculiar attitudes?

Gwen checked her message machines at three that afternoon. One call was from Heather. "Gwen, Mr. Fortune would like you to give Alamo a bath. He got into some mud somewhere, and I guess he's an awful mess. Anyhow, please try to fit it into your schedule today. Thanks."

Gwen's heart was suddenly in her throat. What if she ran into Zane again?

But that was hardly likely to happen, and she shouldn't worry about it. She hadn't yet cut Zane from her client list, so she really must keep up on his requests. Besides, it would only take about thirty minutes to bathe the dog, and every bath meant another fifty dollars in her pocket. She could not afford to ignore Heather's call, or to even pretend that she'd gotten her message too late to do the job today.

Regardless, she drove into Zane's driveway with a wary eye. But the elegant house and grounds looked as they always did when she went there, with no vehicles in sight and no sign of anyone being home. She relaxed some. Parking around back, as usual, she got out and unlocked a side door of the house with her key.

Standing on the threshold with the door open, she called, "Alamo?"

The shepherd came racing through the house, barking happily. Gwen knelt down and petted him, then frowned. "You're not muddy. What in the world was Heather talking about?"

"Hello, Gwen."

At the sound of Zane's voice, she jumped up. "What's going on?"

"I had to see you. There's something we have to discuss. Please come in."

Her eyes sparked angrily. "You had Heather phone with a lie to get me here? Isn't having someone else do your dirty work a new low, even for you? Then again, maybe it's not, since you're so used to having everything your way—"

Zane broke into her tirade. "I have another business proposition to present to you. Would you stop yelling at me long enough to hear what it is?"

"I wasn't yelling," she snapped.

Why did he want her so much? Zane asked himself. What man in his right mind kept aching for a woman who made it so plain that she would prefer him to vanish from the face of the earth? But even her anger and sarcasm excited him. Everything she did excited him. He felt breathless just looking at her.

Gwen had finally tuned in to his "business proposition" remark, and her eyes narrowed suspiciously. She didn't trust Zane. He worried her. He disturbed her. In some ways her life had become more difficult than it had been before meeting him. Prior to his first kiss she'd had no trouble at all with her libido. Now she never knew when a flash of desire might hit her, which she didn't appreciate. But then, laying all the blame on him would be unfair. She hadn't had to kiss him back, after all, or, let him go so far in the theater.

But not one second of intimacy would have occurred between them if she hadn't gone along with his
first business proposition. Why *wouldn't* she be suspicious of whatever it was that he had in mind today?

"What do you want me to help you do now, rob a
bank?" she intoned sardonically.

"Funny," he retorted dryly. "Very funny."

Folding her arms across her chest, she leaned
against the door frame. "If it's so funny, why aren't
you laughing?" Though he'd shed his suit jacket, he
was still wearing office garb, and he looked fabulous,
as usual, which she couldn't help noticing and resenting. He always looked great, and she always looked
like the rag-collector's child. It was probably an overly
dramatic comparison, but it was pretty much how she
felt in her worn jeans and old red shirt.

He hit her with a look of pure frustration. "Would
you please come in so we can shut the door? I promise
not to keep you for more than ten minutes."

"So you can present your business proposition,"
she said with exaggerated sweetness. "If I remember
correctly, ten minutes was what you asked for the first
time you—"

"Dammit, Gwen, I didn't ask you to come here so
we could argue!"

"*You* didn't ask me at all. Your secretary did."

"Would you have come if I'd asked?" he shouted.

She had succeeded in angering him, and was surprised that it gave her no pleasure. Rather, she felt
small and petty for having goaded him.

"All right," she said evenly, striving for an indif-
ference she really didn't feel. "Say your piece. I don't
have time to stand around here for the rest of the day."

"For your information, neither do I." Apparently

she wasn't going to move away from the door, and he wondered if she thought she was going to have to run to protect her virtue.

"Okay," he continued. "Here's the situation. Lily phoned me with an invitation to attend a barbecue at the ranch on Saturday. She mentioned you several times and would like you to go with me. Everyone still believes we're an item, and I'd like to keep it that way. But that's not the whole reason I'm asking you to go. I honestly think you'd enjoy the barbecue. It's mostly a family gathering. Dad throws a barbecue party two or three times every year. Everyone brings their kids, dresses casually and has a great time. It will be much different from Hannah and Parker's wedding, and—"

Gwen held up her hand. "Back up a bit. There are going to be children at the barbecue?" An idea was forming in the back of her mind, one that would put an end to Zane's interest in her for all time.

"Yes," Zane said. "There'll probably be a dozen kids there, maybe more."

"Then I could bring my kids?"

Zane blinked. "If you'd like, yes," he said slowly, realizing that he hadn't considered Gwen's kids when plotting this opportunity to ask her to the affair.

"Okay, fine, I'll go," she said.

"You will?"

"Yes, I will. What time do you want to pick us up on Saturday?"

"Probably around, uh, ten in the morning. That would give us plenty of time for the drive."

She could see that she had discombobulated him. He probably hadn't even thought of her kids, the cad. Fuming, she decided not to let him off the hook this easily. "So, what business proposition did you intend to offer me? Were you planning to pay me for attending the barbecue, like you did for the wedding?"

Zane's neck and face got red. "It crossed my mind, yes."

"I'm sure it did," she drawled cynically.

"But I'm much happier that you'll be going because you want to," Zane said quickly, speaking the truth.

To his surprise she smiled. "Oh, I want to, believe me."

There was something wrong with the way she'd said that, and Zane suddenly wasn't quite as happy about the date as he'd been a second before. It was as though she'd just gotten the upper hand on some point and was gloating about it.

Gwen took a look at her watch. "I have to be going. I'll be ready at ten on Saturday morning."

"Good," Zane said uneasily. "I'll be there."

He stood in the doorway and watched her walk to her van and get in. Perplexity gnawed at his stomach. Gwen was up to something, but what? He wished he could read her better.

After she'd driven away, so did he, and all the way back to the office he tried to figure Gwen out. She had agreed to go to the barbecue with him much, much more easily than he'd thought she would.

The question was, why?

Zane liked kids and wasn't at all concerned about Gwen bringing hers to Saturday's barbecue. But something had definitely changed because of the impending event. Even though she'd told him about her having children, he'd never thought of her as anything but a desirable woman. Now he also thought of her as a mother, which added a respectful depth to his sensual feelings for her. Maybe because he'd lost his own mother at a young age, he had always put motherhood right up there with honor and loyalty to country.

Even so, there was a nasty little fear in the back of his mind about actually seeing Gwen with her kids. Until that occurred, he couldn't be sure that his feelings for her wouldn't take a different turn, and that idea *did* concern him. He liked and wanted Gwen as he knew her now, and he could only guess at how the presence of her children might affect her.

He hoped ardently that she wasn't one of those women who let their kids run wild, and at the same time prayed that she wasn't so protective of them that she followed them around and ruined their fun. There would be pony rides for the younger kids, he knew from past barbecues, and for the first time it occurred to him that he had no idea how old Gwen's children were.

In fact, he realized with a sinking sensation, he knew nothing at all about Gwen's kids—not their names, their ages or even how many she had. Wasn't it rather odd that she hadn't whipped out wallet snapshots for him to look at? Didn't a parent usually do that with even the most casual acquaintance?

Theirs was a strange relationship, Zane had to admit, and then felt upset over the possibility that Gwen might feel that they really had no relationship at all. At least not a genuine one. After all, it had started out on a most peculiar note, with him hiring her to delude his matchmaking sisters.

But he saw tremendous advancement after that because of their undeniable physical attraction for each other. *He* couldn't deny it, at any rate. Could Gwen?

he wondered uneasily. That could be the crux of the animosity she laid on him most of the time.

And he didn't understand why she was so adamantly opposed to dating either. He might as well face it, he thought grimly. He really didn't understand Gwen. No man should become involved with a woman he didn't understand. If that wasn't asking for trouble, what was?

Good Lord, he thought, disgusted with himself, there were dozens, *hundreds* of attractive, sexy, willing women right here in San Antonio. He sure didn't have to beg crumbs from Gwen or any other woman to ensure female companionship. So why didn't he just forget Gwen Hutton and get on with his life?

Because you've never felt this way about a woman before. She was the first woman since Melanie Wilson that he could not get out of his system, no matter what he did or how hard he tried.

Damn, he thought angrily, if he was stupid enough to want another woman who couldn't love him, then he deserved to suffer.

His spine stiffened. He would not suffer indefinitely. The barbecue was going to be it. If Gwen continued to shut him out on Saturday, then it was over for them.

It was an oath he intended to keep.

Around five that afternoon Gwen arrived at Ramona's to pick up her kids. After a few moments of ordinary chitchat, Gwen said nonchalantly, "Could I borrow Tommy and Liselle on Saturday?"

Ramona's jaw dropped. "You want to borrow my kids?"

Gwen grinned. "Yes, and they'll probably have the time of their lives. You see, Zane asked me to attend a family barbecue at the Double Crown Ranch. He said that everyone will be bringing their children, so I'm taking my three and I know they'd be thrilled if Tommy and Liselle came with us. What do you say? I promise to watch them very closely.''

"Tommy and Liselle would be in seventh heaven at an outing like that, and I know you would take very good care of them. But, goodness, five small children at one time just might scare Zane to death.''

Gwen smiled again. "I'm sure it will.''

Ramona's eyes widened as understanding struck her. "That's what you'd like to happen! For heaven's sake, why?''

Gwen was no longer smiling. Instead, resentment began burning in her eyes. "Because he's a self-centered jerk and deserves a dose of reality more than anyone I've ever met. Not once has he mentioned my kids, even though I told him I'm a mother. He hasn't asked their ages, or even how many children I have. Anyhow, you and I know there's no more definitive reality than small kids—their noise, the demands they make on your time, the almost constant attention they require.''

Even though Gwen seemed deadly serious, Ramona couldn't help laughing. "Well, five little kids for a day would be one way of shocking the socks off the man, but are you sure you want to do that? Gwen, Zane Fortune is quite a catch, and he seems to like you.''

Gwen sniffed derogatorily. "Zane likes women, period. I mean no more to him than any other woman, and he'd take me to bed in a minute if I let him, same as he's done all his adult life with any available female. Ramona, for a person like me Zane is heartache waiting to happen. I'm simply not in the market for that kind of pain.''

Ramona looked worried. "I know you're not, but I still can't help feeling that you might be missing the boat with Zane. Are you positive you're not misjudging him? For example, why would he invite you to that barbecue? That sort of affair is hardly conducive to seduction, if that's all he has in mind."

"Ramona, you're forgetting that he paid me to go to that wedding with him. His family still thinks we're a couple. He told me straight out that he'd like to keep them believing it. Really, that's all there is to his attention."

Ramona cleared her throat. "Has...has he actually tried to take you to bed?"

"Practically," Gwen mumbled, recalling the theater incident with sufficient embarrassment to redden her cheeks. She drew a breath to even out her suddenly racing pulse. That memory never failed to unnerve her.

"Ramona, the bottom line is that I'm not experienced enough to deal with a man of Zane's caliber and I'd like him to leave me entirely alone. I've even considered crossing him off my client list, and you know how I value each and every client. Anyway, when he asked me to the barbecue and mentioned the children that would be there, I decided it was time he met *my* kids."

"And, apparently, mine," Ramona said quietly.

"The more the merrier," Gwen said flatly. "So, is it all right if I take Tommy and Liselle on Saturday?"

Ramona nodded. "Yes, of course. I know that Tommy, especially, would love to see a real working ranch. He's crazy about horses."

"So is Donnie. Okay, great. Could you bring them over to my house around nine-thirty on Saturday morning? And dress them in jeans or something else comfortable.''

''Will do.''

But later Gwen too kept having second thoughts about Saturday. When Zane had mentioned children attending the barbecue, she had responded impulsively, immediately certain that a long day with small kids to care for would cool any foolish romantic ideas Zane had about the two of them.

But thinking about how her kids might take seeing her with a man had started bothering her something awful. Since their daddy, who Donnie and Ashley remembered, there had been no men for them *to* see. Gwen wasn't sure if they were old enough to resent another man with their mommy, or just what their reaction would be to Zane. Maybe there'd be no reaction at all. But if there was, how would she handle it?

She must prepare them ahead of time, she decided, so after baths that night she sat them down on Donnie's bed for a talk.

''I have something to tell you,'' she said, looking at each shiny-clean, beautiful little face gazing back at her. She loved them so much, and she knew they loved her. They also loved their grandparents. But she was their mainstay, their mother, and while they were young, they would love her best. She could never hurt them in any way, and she would wear herself out working to support and care for them, if that's what it took.

She kept her voice even and gentle. ''We've been invited to a barbecue at a ranch on Saturday,'' she said.

''Us too?'' Donnie asked, instantly excited.

"Yes, all of us. A man I know invited us. His name is Zane Fortune."

"Is it a real ranch?" Donnie asked excitedly.

"Yes, it's a real ranch. About Mr. Fortune—"

"With horses and cowboys, Mom?"

Ashley piped up. "Could we ride the horses, Mommy?"

Tiny Mindy echoed, "Ride horsies, Mommy?"

"I don't know about riding the horses, kids, but I'm pretty sure you will be able to see them. About Mr. Fortune—"

"I bet the *boys* will be able to ride the horses," Donnie said with a superior look at his sisters. "Hey, Mom, will there be other boys there?"

"Yes. In fact, I'm taking Tommy and Liselle with us, so Tommy will be there for sure."

"Yay!" the three shouted, almost in unison.

Gwen looked at her three children with no small feeling of dismay. They weren't one bit interested in hearing anything about Zane. What mere man could compete with a real ranch and the possibility of riding a horse?

But when they actually met Zane, and saw him as a flesh-and-blood man, and realized that he was Mommy's friend, how would they feel then?

Gwen sighed, then made herself smile at her precious children. "So, we'll go to the barbecue with Mr. Fortune, right?"

"Yes!" Donnie cried, and bounced up and down on the bed. "Yes!" Ashley said, and took a few bounces herself. Mindy merely bounced and giggled.

Gwen got up. "Okay, time for prayers."

"Mom, how many days till Saturday?" Donnie asked.

"Two, sweetheart."

His little face fell. "Two whole days? Gee whiz."

"Hey, none of that. Two days are hardly anything. They'll go by so fast that Saturday will be here before you know it."

Only after prayers, kisses and good-nights, did Gwen lay in her own bed and realize how true that was.

Nine

Gwen had all five children lined up on the couch before ten on Saturday morning. They were adorable, dressed in jeans and colorful tops, and too excited to sit completely still, though they tried because of Gwen's watchful eye.

"We don't want anyone getting dirty or mussed, so we're all going to just sit and wait for Mr. Fortune," she told them, taking a chair herself. She too wore jeans—her best pair—and a favorite red-and-white checked shirt. Her long hair was drawn back from her face in a French braid, and she had put on a little makeup. Everything was ready to go.

Everything but her nerves, that is. Try as she might, she could not settle them—they were jumping around like popping corn. Why on earth was she putting herself through this? she thought rather frantically, even while smiling lovingly at the children on the couch. Juggling five small kids, Zane and the rest of the Fortune family all day was probably going to turn her into a basket case.

Well, no, of course it wouldn't do that. She would cope, as she always did. But couldn't she have come up with an easier way to discourage Zane's purely sexual interest?

But she'd told him more than once that she wasn't interested, so he was obviously one of those people who didn't understand the word *no*. On the other hand, would any man believe a woman who said no and then kissed back as though starved for affection? Gwen frowned. Maybe she *was* starved for affection. If not, why would she have let Zane go so far in the theater?

But that had not been ordinary affection, that had been…it had been…

Flushing hotly, she smiled at the kids again. "Mr. Fortune should be here any minute. You are all being very good. I'm proud of you. Now remember, you are to also sit still in his car, and please don't yell or tease each other during the drive to the ranch. I'm sure that once we're there, you'll be able to run and play and have lots of fun."

"And ride the horses," Donnie said.

"I made no promises about that, son," Gwen said.

"But if they have horses, Mom, why wouldn't they let people ride 'em?"

"Maybe they will. But there's also a chance that they don't want strangers riding their horses. We're just going to have to wait and see, Donnie."

The doorbell rang, and Gwen nearly jumped out of her skin. "That's probably Mr. Fortune," she said to the children as she got up from her chair. "Now, I'd like you all to sit very still while I let him in. Then I will introduce you, and I'd like each of you to say hello when I say your name, all right?"

The kids agreed in varying ways, and Gwen sucked in a nervous breath and hurried to the door. When she opened it, Zane was smiling. "Good morning," he said cheerfully. "Ready to go?"

"Good morning," she replied. "We're ready, but please come in and meet the children first."

"Yes, that's probably a good idea." Zane had told

himself all the way from his house that Gwen was Gwen, and that worrying about seeing her with her children was ridiculous. She looked beautiful this morning, bright-eyed and young and so desirable. He couldn't help wishing that they were going off by themselves to be alone somewhere, but…she had kids, and he'd better get along with them if he wanted to get anywhere with their mother. He strongly suspected that if her kids didn't like him, then neither would Gwen.

Still, when she opened the door for him, and he saw five small children seated on the sofa, he nearly swallowed his tongue.

"You have…five children?" he said weakly.

Gwen saw his suddenly ashen color and knew that she'd done what she'd planned to do. Zane was shocked and looked ready to run. But her heart skipped a beat as she suddenly realized that she didn't *want* him to run.

She cleared her clogged throat. "Three are mine— the towheads. Let me introduce you. Kids, this is Mr. Zane Fortune. Zane, this is Tommy, Donnie, Liselle, Mindy and Ashley. Tommy and Liselle belong to a friend of mind."

Each child said a shy hello. Zane said hello, and he tried to put on a face that would appeal to children. They merely stared up at him, as only young children can do, with total innocence and no embarrassment. And they were beautiful children, all five of them, even the two who weren't Gwen's.

Zane felt something release inside himself, undoubtedly the tension he'd been suffering over seeing Gwen with her kids. Out of the corner of his eye he saw her standing very still and watching. Had she been worrying also, wondering how he would react to this moment? Wondering how the kids would react? Inviting her friend's two children to increase the number of childish eyes giving him the once-over had to be some kind of test, he decided. Was he passing it?

Then he realized that he felt amazingly good, and he wanted Gwen to know that his initial surprise had vanished. He looked at her and smiled. "You have beautiful children."

She looked startled, but only for a moment. "Thank you."

Zane's gaze returned to the kids. "Well, is everyone ready to go?" The kids all nodded. "This is going to be a fun day," Zane said. "There'll be other kids to play with at the ranch, and lots of good food, and pony rides."

Donnie's eyes got big with excitement. "Told you so, Mom!"

"Yes, you did, son. All right, everyone up." Before she had finished her sentence, the kids were off the sofa and racing for the door, with Mindy trying to keep up with the others. "Slow down," Gwen said sternly. "Ashley, please take Mindy's hand."

"Yes, Mommy." Ashley took her baby sister's hand, and the group filed outside in a more orderly fashion.

Zane grinned at Gwen. "They're great, Gwen, just great."

"If you can still say that at the end of the day, then I'll believe you mean it."

Gwen kept the kids occupied during the drive with stories and songs. It amazed her when Zane sang along, loudly and sometimes off-key, but he seemed to be perfectly at ease with a sports utility vehicle full of youngsters, and that too surprised her. Apparently he was much more adaptable than she'd given him credit for. In fact, before they reached the ranch she started wondering if Ramona had been more right than wrong when she'd said that Gwen could be misjudging Zane's intentions.

On the other hand, his good humor could merely be a darn good act. Dare she forget how capable he was of deluding people? Even his own family?

Either way, Zane was a Fortune, a man of incredible wealth from a family of billionaires. He was highly educated and had lived with opulence since the day of his birth. Why would he even look twice at her? She hadn't finished college, and she certainly wasn't a ravishing beauty. On top of that she had three kids to raise.

And so she deduced again that he could want only one thing from her, which made her eyes and nose sting, warning her that tears were much too close. To keep them at bay she started another song, and the kids and Zane joined in. Hearing him singing, "Mary Had a Little Lamb," caused her to laugh, and he sent her a grin that tore at her heartstrings.

Sighing to herself, Gwen worried about what she was getting herself into. Obviously she'd made a bad mistake by agreeing to today's event. Truth be told, she'd done little else *but* make mistakes since meeting Zane.

And all for two thousand dollars she couldn't even spend.

When the song was over, she didn't immediately start another. Instead she quietly asked Zane, "Have you had your car repaired yet?"

Her question took him by surprise, and he hemmed

and hawed for a second, then perpetuated his lie by saying, "Not yet."

She could not keep still on this matter any longer. She needed that money and resented his procrastination. The look she laid on him wasn't very kind. "You probably don't understand," she said sharply, "but until I pay for those repairs I won't know if there'll be anything left of the two thousand I banked after your friends' wedding."

Zane sent her a startled look. It hadn't occurred to him that she would save that money to pay for the repairs to his car. He felt rather foolish for ever thinking that she would never find out that he'd taken care of the whole thing himself.

Looking out the windshield again, he heaved a sigh. "Guess it's truth time."

"What's that supposed to mean?" Gwen asked suspiciously. What lie had he told her that was now catching up with him? Was he constantly hiding something from someone? She'd never liked lies or liars, and it hurt her heart to think that Zane might have lied her. True, she'd gone along with his lie at the wedding, which really had been a lousy trick to pull on his family. But it hadn't entered her mind that the wedding scam might be something more than an isolated incident. A prank of sorts. By heavens, she thought, suddenly passionate about her role in Zane's deception, she was *not* going to tell one single lie to one single person today. Zane could like it or lump it.

"The car was repaired right away," he said quietly, without looking at her. "I didn't tell you about it because I didn't want you insisting on paying the bill."

Gwen stared at him, momentarily speechless, and was just about to make some sort of objection when she heard Tommy and Donnie squabbling in the back. Each boy was certain that he would be the first to take a pony ride.

Angry at Zane, Gwen turned around with a fierce expression. "If I hear one more word of argument out of you boys, neither if you will be taking a pony ride. Do you understand?"

"Yes, Mom," Donnie said meekly.

"Yes, Gwen," Tommy said quietly.

Gwen turned her gaze back to Zane. "Now, you and I are not going to do any debating in front of the kids, but the subject we were discussing is far from closed."

"It's closed as far as I'm concerned," Zane said flatly. "The car is fixed, and I paid for it. That's the end of it."

"It's *not* the end of it," she retorted furiously, but quietly so the kids wouldn't hear them. "I pay my own bills, and I don't appreciate—"

"Gwen, just drop it," Zane snapped. "We were all having fun. Don't ruin the day with a ridiculous argument over something so trivial."

"It's not trivial to me," she fumed.

"Fine, you got the last word. Now can we drop it? Hey, kids," he called. "We're almost to the ranch. And boys, there's more than one pony. You both can ride at the same time, I promise."

Gwen drew a breath and did her best to force her body to relax. The kids were eagerly looking forward to the day, and she truly wanted them to enjoy themselves. Her problems with Zane could be put aside until a later time. Just when that would be, Gwen didn't know, but maybe she shouldn't be worrying about it now.

But his insistence on paying for the car repairs
rubbed her wrong. She paid her own way in this world,
and she didn't like being treated like a charity case. It
was something she was going to have to tell him. In
fact, she probably wouldn't even completely be at ease
until she told him that—and possibly a few other
things.

She would, however, make the best of the barbecue.
Maybe an opportunity for a frank discussion would
present itself when he brought them home after the
event was over. All she could do was to wait and see.

The Fortune family at play was a sight to behold.
Gwen was amazed at how different this gathering was
from the formal wedding. Everyone was in comfortable clothing and totally relaxed, sitting around on
lawn furniture, sipping soft drinks or beer, telling
jokes, wisecracking, teasing each other and doing a lot
of laughing.

She'd been greeted warmly and made to feel at
home. She'd noticed a few surprised faces over her
having children, but that passed quickly, especially after she'd explained that only three of the five were
hers.

The kids were having a ball. The mothers in the
group—and several nannies, Gwen realized—kept an
eye on the children while they romped on the grass,
but then the men took over and began overseeing the
pony rides.

Vanessa moved her chair next to Gwen's. "Zane
didn't mention your children, Gwen," she said. "I'm
so glad you brought them. They're sweet, beautiful
kids."

Gwen smiled. "Thank you. They're having a lot of fun here today."

"I hope so. Gwen, please don't think of me as nosy, but I can't help being curious. The children's father…"

"I'm a widow," Gwen said quietly.

With a sympathetic expression Vanessa laid her hand on Gwen's arm. "I'm so sorry," she said gently.

Gwen looked at Zane's sister and smiled softly. "Thank you, you're very kind."

"I'm also very pleased that Zane seems to be settling down. Zane knows how I feel about this, so I'm not saying anything to you that I wouldn't say to his face. And this change in him is all because of you, Gwen."

Remembering her vow not to lie to these people today, Gwen frowned. "You mustn't misunderstand Zane's and my relationship, Vanessa. We're really just friends."

Vanessa laughed gaily. "Gwen, my dear, Zane does not have female friends. At least, to my knowledge he never has before. No, I can't help believing that he cares a great deal for you. At the risk of being blunt, I doubt that you'd be here today if he didn't. Over the years he's rarely brought a woman to a family function, and within a very short time he's brought you to two affairs. That's really quite revealing, Gwen."

Gwen's heart sank. Her presence alone was reinforcing Zane's lie, and how could she deny it without looking bad herself? She had, after all, accepted money for helping Zane delude his family. If she told the truth now, Vanessa—and probably every other family member—would be thunderstruck. Certainly they wouldn't forgive her, and they might even turn on Zane.

Feeling a bit panicky, her gaze went to Zane and the group of men and children near the corral where the pony rides were taking place. To her surprise, Zane was holding Mindy, who was one of the smallest, youngest children at the barbecue—except for the infants who were either in their mother's or nanny's arms, or sleeping in buggies or infant carriers close by. Even from a distance Gwen could tell that tiny Mindy was perfectly at ease in Zane's arms, and an overwhelming weakness suddenly sapped Gwen's strength. If Zane could charm Mindy, who shied from strangers, he could charm anyone.

"The food's almost ready," Lily announced as she returned from checking on the progress of the beef being barbecued.

At that very moment Gwen heard Ashley let out a screech. Chilled by the sound of her daughter's voice, Gwen saw Zane hastily hand Mindy to his brother Dallas and then disappear into the corral.

All but leaping out of her chair, Gwen took off running. "Ashley…Zane?" she yelled as she ran, and arrived at the corral out of breath.

"She took a fall," Dallas told her with a concerned frown.

"Oh, no," Gwen moaned as she spotted the bleeding gash on Ashley's forehead. Entering the corral, she knelt beside the little girl. Zane was on Ashley's other side, trying to stop the bleeding with his handkerchief.

His eyes rose to meet Gwen's, and he looked anguished. "I think she needs stitches, Gwen. I'm so sorry."

"Where's the nearest hospital?" Gwen asked anxiously.

"In Red Rock." Zane picked up Ashley and got to his feet. "Come on, let's get going."

They raced toward his car. Ashley, in Zane's arms, had stopped wailing, which frightened Gwen more than her crying had. Everyone at the affair was milling about and looking worried. Several people called out that they would watch the other kids while Gwen and Zane were gone, and Gwen called back a grateful, if hasty "thanks."

Gwen got in the front seat and Zane laid the child on her lap. Then he bounded around to the driver's side, got in and immediately started the engine. He drove away fast while Gwen pressed the handkerchief to the gash on her little daughter's forehead.

"Head wounds bleed worse than others," she said unsteadily, trying to maintain her equilibrium.

"Yes, they do," Zane agreed, keeping his eyes on the road because of the speed he was driving. "Gwen, I'm so damn sorry. I should have been watching her more closely."

"What happened?"

"She fell off the pony and hit her head on a corral post. One second she was doing great, and the next she was on the ground. I have no idea why she fell."

"It's not your fault," Gwen said quietly. "These things happen with children." Glancing at Zane, her heart went out to him. He looked stricken. "I mean it, Zane. It wasn't your fault."

Zane sent her a confused look. Why was she being so nice about this when she'd lambasted the hell out of him for a lot less?

They didn't talk for the rest of the drive, not to each

other, at any rate. Gwen kept murmuring comforting words to her little girl, getting Ashley to keep saying things back to her so the child wouldn't fall asleep.

At the hospital in Red Rock, Zane drove up to the Emergency Room door, jumped out of the car and ran around to open Gwen's door. Carrying Ashley, he ran into the hospital and shouted, "This child has a head injury!"

A nurse appeared and led them through another set of doors, where she told Zane to lay the child on the bed behind curtain number two. She pulled the bloody handkerchief away from the gash and looked at it, then pressed a sterile pad to the cut, then told Zane to hold it in place. She said she would notify the doctor on duty, and hurried away.

Gwen's legs suddenly felt rubbery, and she sank onto a stool next to the bed. The cut was only about an inch wide, but it was still bleeding, although the flow had definitely slowed. Regardless, just the thought of so much blood pumping out of her little daughter made Gwen feel queasy.

But she put on a brave face for Ashley and held her hand. Zane, she saw, was holding Ashley's other hand. He was, in fact, behaving like a concerned father, and something about the strength he conveyed helped to calm Gwen.

"Will they give me a shot, Mommy?" Ashley asked in a quivery voice.

"I don't know what the doctor will do, sweetheart," Gwen said. "But whatever it is, I'll be right here beside you. And both of us must be very brave and strong. You're a brave girl, aren't you?"

"Yes, Mommy," the child whispered.

A man in a white coat came in. "I'm Dr. Parker. What's the child's name?

"Ashley," Gwen said.

Zane stepped away from the bed, and Dr. Parker took his place. "Hello, Ashley. I'm going to examine your injury." Gently he lifted the pad. "How did you get hurt?"

"I fell off the pony."

Dr. Parker looked at Zane. "You're Ashley's father?"

"No, but Gwen Hutton here is her mother. I'm Zane Fortune. The accident happened at the Double Crown Ranch."

A woman came in, and looked at both Zane and Gwen. "Are you the child's parents?"

Gwen answered before Zane could. "I'm her mother."

"Would you come with me, please? We need to fill out a few forms."

Gwen sent Ashley a worried look, and Dr. Parker intervened. "Go ahead, Gwen. You too, Mr. Fortune. Ashley and I will get along just fine."

Reluctantly Gwen followed the woman, and felt a little better when Zane took her arm and said quietly, "She'll be okay, Gwen."

"Yes, I know that now, but she's little more than a baby, and she's frightened."

Having reached an office alcove, the woman turned and smiled at them. "Dr. Parker is wonderful with children. I know you can't help worrying, but your daughter is in very good hands. Please have a seat." Seating herself, the woman took out several forms.

Gwen and Zane sat across the counter from her, and when Zane reached for Gwen's hand, she let him hold it. She realized how good it felt to have a man at her side at a time like this.

"Your name, please?" the woman asked with a pen poised above the first form.

"Gwen Hutton."

"Address?"

The questions continued. Gwen answered and the woman wrote.

"Do you have medical insurance?" the woman asked.

"No," Gwen said quietly. "But I have my checkbook with me, and I'll take care of the bill."

Zane could hardly believe what he'd just heard. With three young children, Gwen had no medical coverage? Was she that badly off financially that she couldn't afford something so crucial? No car insurance, and now this. My God, he thought sorrowfully, how she must worry. His hands clenched into fists as he pondered the inequities of life. He'd never gone without, and Gwen lived and raised her kids without so many things. Forget the luxuries that made life good, Gwen didn't even have the necessities.

When the woman's phone rang and she answered it, Zane whispered, "Gwen, would you let me pay this bill?"

Gwen sent him a quick, startled look and shook her head. "I can cover it, but thank you for offering."

"Gwen, I have so much and you—"

"Stop," she whispered. "What you have has nothing to do with me."

"But—"

"No buts, Zane. That's just the way it is."

He sat there and felt miserable while the woman and Gwen finished the paperwork.

He felt guilty for having so much while good, hard-working people like Gwen barely got by. The Fortune family was traditionally generous with numerous charities, but there was always more a person could do. He wished passionately that Gwen would let him do something for her, let him help her out with money that he would never miss.

But in his heart he knew that she would never take an unearned cent from him or anyone else. She had as much pride as she did spunk, and she paid her own way. And he couldn't help admiring her for it.

Ten

It seemed to take forever in the Emergency Room. Dr. Parker was an extremely thorough physician, and he closely checked Ashley for other injuries. "A fall from a horse can be serious business," he told Gwen. To her intense relief, however, beyond the cut on Ashley's forehead he found nothing but some bruises.

Still, after he finally stitched Ashley's forehead, he then requested that she remain lying down for a while so he could keep an eye on her. Naturally Gwen and Zane didn't say no. They had put the little girl in Dr. Parker's hands, and they would not rush his treatment. Gwen sat next to her daughter's bed for hours, and Zane did a lot of pacing in the waiting room, though every so often he would appear to see for himself how Ashley was doing.

His concern seemed so genuine to Gwen, and she kept thinking of that while she watched Ashley and held her hand. There were more sides to Zane than she could have guessed.

Much later Zane slipped in to the curtained cubicle and whispered, "How's she doing?"

"Okay," Gwen whispered back. The dried blood on his shirt bothered her every time she saw it, but her own blouse—and Ashley's clothes—had the same dark stains. She would soak her and Ashley's things and try to save them, but Zane would probably toss his shirt in the trash can. As trivial as discarding a few clothes was in the greater scheme of things, it illustrated quite graphically just how far apart in thought and deed she and Zane really were.

And if she wanted further proof of their incompatibility, all she had to do was look at him. He was handsome beyond belief, a golden-haired Adonis, and she was…she was… Well, she certainly wasn't in his league in the looks department. She wasn't in his league in *any* department, so why did he even bother with her? Wasn't assuming that he was pining for her body just a bit far-fetched when he could probably have any woman he wanted?

"Has the doctor been in again?" Zane whispered.

"He took a quick look and rushed out. He seems to be very busy, but I'm sure he'll let us know when he thinks it's safe for Ashley to leave."

"Yes, I'm sure he will. Gwen, are you holding up okay?"

"Yes, don't worry about me."

There was that tough note of independence again, Zane thought. Had she always been this way, determined to take care of herself, by herself? What kind of man had her husband been? Had she been the strong one in that relationship? And what about her folks? Had they raised her to rely on no one but herself?

He looked into her eyes and again wished she would let him help her out financially. But he knew it wasn't going to happen. He would give her what she would accept—moral support.

"All right," he said quietly, with an ache in his heart, "I'll take another stroll around."

Watching him walk out of the curtained cubicle, Gwen suddenly recalled Rosita Perez's prediction at

Hannah and Parker's wedding. It would mean nothing at all to Gwen if Zane hadn't told her later on that Rosita's prophesies often came true, and that people in the area had come to respect them.

"But she said such ridiculous things," Gwen mumbled under her breath. Rosita must be dead wrong. Maybe someday Gwen would run into Rosita again and tell her so.

The sun was low on the western horizon when they finally got back to the ranch. No one was outside, so obviously the barbecue was over and everyone had either left or was inside the big house.

Ashley was sleeping in her mother's arms, and Zane spoke quietly as he turned off the ignition. "Don't disturb her. Stay here and I'll round up the other kids."

"Thank you. Please thank your family for me too."

"Will do." Zane got out and very quietly shut the door.

A few moments after he went into Ryan Fortune's fabulous house, Lily came out. Gwen saw the wicker basket Lily was carrying and suspected what it contained. Lily walked up to the passenger side of the car, and Gwen rolled down the window.

"Zane told us she's all right," Lily said in an undertone when she saw that Ashley was asleep. "I'm so sorry she got hurt, Gwen. I hope it didn't upset you too much. I raised three children myself, and I did my share of Emergency Room duty, as most mothers do." Lily gazed fondly at the sleeping child. "She's a lovely little girl, and your other two are marvelous children. Mindy captured everyone's heart today, and

Donnie is a very bright, handsome little boy. You must be very proud of all three.''

"I am, Lily, thank you.''

"And Zane seems to sincerely care about your children.''

Gwen couldn't deny Lily's observation, yet it made her strangely uneasy. She smiled and nodded, but couldn't quite bring herself to agree with Lily's comment.

"Oh, here he comes now, with the children,'' Lily said, looking toward the house.

Gwen turned her eyes and saw Zane carrying Mindy again. The other kids all but encircled his legs, and Gwen was surprised that they didn't run ahead to the car. Why, Zane looks like a...father! she thought, and her heart was suddenly beating erratically.

"I'm going to put this basket in the back,'' Lily said. "Ryan's barbecued beef is very special, and I wanted you to have some.''

"That's very nice of you, Lily. Thank you.''

"You're welcome, Gwen, and do come to the ranch again. You and your children have an open invitation.'' Lily smiled warmly. "Even your two little guests were well-behaved.''

Gwen smiled too. "Their mother will be pleased to hear that.'' Zane was getting the kids settled in the back seat, making sure their seat belts were buckled.

"Mom, did Ash get sewed up?'' Donnie called.

"Yes, son, she has five tiny stitches.''

"Can I see 'em?''

"She has a bandage, Donnie. You can see them tomorrow.'' Zane was getting behind the wheel, and Gwen looked at Lily again. "Thank you for everything, Lily, especially for watching the other kids while I was gone with Ashley.''

"It was my pleasure, Gwen. Take care. Zane, we hope to see you again real soon. Goodbye, and drive safely.'' Lily waved at the kids in the back seat, then moved away from the car.

Zane said goodbye, put the vehicle in gear and drove away.

There was very little conversation during the drive from the ranch to San Antonio. Mindy was sound asleep moments later. The other children in the back seat were quiet and subdued, and Gwen knew that they had had a big day and were tired. Without songs and childish laughter, the trip home was much different from the one to the ranch earlier that day.

Night had fallen before they reached the city. Gwen's arms ached from holding Ashley for so long, and she was glad when they were finally in San Antonio. Her initial plan had been to have Zane drop her and the kids at her house, then she would drive Tommy and Liselle to their own home. But now, getting close to her neighborhood, she came up with a new and, given the circumstances, more sensible plan.

"Zane, would you mind driving to my friend's house to drop off Tommy and Liselle?''

"Not at all. Give me the address and directions.''

Gwen recited both, and Zane drove directly to Ramona's house and pulled into her driveway. "I'll take the kids in so you won't have to wake up Ashley and Mindy.''

"Thanks, I'd appreciate that,'' Gwen said quietly. Zane had surprised her all day with his patience, his kindness, his helpfulness.

Gwen sighed as he got out and opened one of the

back doors for Tommy and Liselle to get out, and she watched him walk the two children to their front door with regret gnawing at her. She'd actually believed the kids would daunt Zane, and had invited Tommy and Liselle along to further overwhelm him. It hadn't worked, and now she was sorry for her own childish behavior.

An outside light was on, illuminating a small porch and most of the driveway. Ramona opened the door before Zane and the kids reached it. Zane smiled at her. "Hello, I'm Zane Fortune."

"I'm Ramona Garcia." She offered her hand for a handshake and said, "Nice meeting you, Zane." Then she looked at the car—as her kids walked past her—and saw Gwen wave at her.

Zane could tell by Ramona's expression that she knew something was wrong, so he explained. "Ashley took a fall and cut her head. She's asleep on Gwen's lap, so I volunteered to deliver Tommy and Liselle."

"That was thoughtful," Ramona murmured with a frown, then hurried from the porch to the car.

Gwen rolled down her window. "She's fine, Ramona," Gwen whispered.

Ramona peered into the car to see for herself. "Call me later," she whispered.

"As soon as I can," Gwen promised.

Zane got in and backed his vehicle from Ramona's driveway.

Gwen gave him instructions on the shortest route to her address from that point, and they were there in five minutes. Never had her little house looked better to her than it did when Zane drove into her driveway.

He turned off the engine. "I've got everything organized," he said. "Give Donnie your house key so he can run ahead and unlock the door. You carry Ashley in, and I'll carry Mindy.''

"Fine,'' Gwen agreed cautiously, so she wouldn't wake Ashley. She dug into her purse for her key ring, which she handed to her son. "Unlock the door and leave it open, Donnie. We'll bring in the girls.''

"Okay, Mom.''

Zane got out first and let Donnie climb out second. Gwen could tell from the way Donnie walked that he, too, was worn out. It had been a long day for all of them.

Then Zane opened the door for her to get out, then undid the seat belt around Mindy and picked her up.

Gwen followed Zane to the house, and they went inside. He let her precede him so she could show him where to lay Mindy down. She brought him to a bedroom with a small bed and a crib—obviously the girls' room. Without speaking a word, they got the girls settled in their beds, removing only their shoes and covering them with blankets. When they returned to the living room, they found Donnie slumped on the sofa.

"Son, did you eat?'' Gwen asked.

"I ate a lot, Mom. It was really good.''

"In that case, please go to your room and get into your pajamas. We're skipping baths tonight. I'll be in later to hear your prayers and tuck you in.''

"Okay,'' the boy said, and slowly got up and shuffled from the room.

"He's done in,'' Gwen said.

"They're *all* done in,'' Zane said, then added, "I'm going to bring in the basket Lily put in the car.''

He was gone before Gwen could tell him to just take the basket home with him, so she put that idea aside and went to Donnie's room. He had undressed down to his underwear, but his pajamas were still on the foot of the bed. He was sound asleep.

"You're one tired little guy, aren't you, sweetheart?" she murmured lovingly, and gently got him under his blankets. Then she hurried to her own bedroom and put on a clean blouse. She had nothing to offer Zane to replace his blood-encrusted shirt, but she reasoned that he would be leaving soon, anyway.

When she returned to the living room she could hear Zane in the kitchen. Walking in, she stopped in surprise. Obviously he didn't intend to leave before they ate. He had laid out the food from the wicker basket, and there was a lot more than just some barbecued beef. And he'd taken off his soiled shirt and was wearing a very sexy plain white undershirt that revealed his broad shoulders and muscular upper arms.

"My goodness," Gwen exclaimed, flustered over Zane's upper body. "Lily packed a feast." There was a pile of barbecued beef sandwiches on huge buns, and plastic containers of coleslaw, Texas-style beans and apple cobbler.

Zane grinned. "Hope you're hungry. I sure am."

How could she possibly object to his staying and eating with her? After all he'd done for her and the kids today, she would be an absolute ingrate if she was anything but gracious.

"Does anything need warming?" she asked. "I have a small microwave."

"The sandwiches and beans should be warmed up."

Gwen took two of the sandwiches and brought them to her counter microwave. "What would you like to drink? I think there are some sodas in the fridge. Or I could make coffee."

"I would love a cup of coffee, if it's not too much trouble."

"It's no trouble at all." Gwen prepared the pot. Her nerves had settled down some; after all, this wasn't the first time she'd seen a man in his undershirt!

When everything was ready, they sat at the table to eat. After only a few bites Gwen murmured, "This is delicious." She hadn't realized how hungry she'd gotten, and from the way Zane was eating, he was in the same condition.

They ate in silence for a few minutes, then Gwen said, "I owe you a world of thanks, Zane. You were wonderful with Ashley. The other kids too."

He sent her a knowing glance. "Which you didn't expect, did you?"

"Well…no," she admitted uneasily. "I mean, with your being a bachelor and all, I really didn't know how you would react to a bunch of kids."

"It was a test, wasn't it?"

Gwen felt heat in her cheeks, but she couldn't lie about it. "Yes, I guess it was," she replied. "But have you figured out why I even thought of testing you?"

"No, can't say that I have."

"It was because I told you almost right away that I had children, and you never asked one single question about them—not how many kids I had or how old they were, or anything else."

Their eyes locked across the table for a long time, then Zane gave in gracefully. "You're right. I thought of you a lot, but never as a mother until you asked if you could bring your kids to the barbecue. I did some thinking about them then. Some wondering."

"All right, I can accept that, but why did you think of me at all?" A defiance gleamed in Gwen's eyes as she wondered if he had the courage to be honest with her.

Zane's immediate response to her challenging question was a short laugh, followed by, "Why does any man think of a particular woman?"

"Hormones?" she said dryly.

"Well, yes, I suppose so," Zane said slowly. "But that's not the extent of it with us. I mean, our relationship didn't start with my chasing you around the house, or vice versa."

"No, it started with my chasing Alamo around the house." Looking into his eyes across the table, she took a bite of her sandwich. Her expression was still challenging. After swallowing, she said, "It actually started with your hiring me to play a dirty trick on your family."

"I was only trying to protect myself from some heavy-duty matchmaking. It worked too."

"Maybe a little too well. I think your family likes me."

"I think the same thing. Does that make you uncomfortable?"

"It makes me feel like a sneak and a liar, because I like them too. Do you want to know the real truth? I wish I had turned you down that day." She sighed, narrowed her eyes a bit, then added, "But I didn't, and if that had been the end of it I might not feel so darn guilty. But that wasn't the end of it, and I'm still deceiving some very nice people. So are you. Doesn't that bother you?"

Zane continued eating, but he was also thinking. "I don't believe we did any deceiving today," he finally stated. "In fact, I think our little deception really only lasted for one day—for Parker and Hannah's wedding.''

"Are you deliberately being obtuse? Zane, Vanessa wants me to be her friend, and Lily issued an open invitation for me and the kids to visit the ranch. They honestly believe that you and I...that we are...'' She stopped to clear her throat.

Zane jumped in. "Are you trying to say that they believe we're lovers?" He set down his fork.

Gwen flushed, but she kept her gaze steady. "Oh, they definitely believe that. Actually, it wouldn't surprise me if they thought our relationship was—'' it was a hard word to say, but she got it out "—serious.''

Frowning slightly, Zane sat back and looked at her. Before he could formulate a reply that made any sense, however, she started talking again.

"And it never could be anything more than it is right now. In fact, I can't help wondering how things even got this far when we're so different from each other. We live in different worlds, and if there are any similarities in our personalities I've yet to find them. So I guess that takes me back to my original question. Why do you think of me at all?''

"Are you saying you never think of me? Not in any context?''

"Would it shatter your ego if I said no?''

Frustration suddenly creased Zane's forehead. "You're damn good at evasion.''

"And you're not?''

"Okay. You want an answer? Here it is.'' Getting up, Zane walked around the table, ignored the startled look on her face, took her hand and brought her to her feet. "Try this on for size,'' he whispered as his arms went around her and his mouth covered hers.

Gwen's head was instantly spinning. Obviously her resistance to Zane's kisses was nil, because, as before, within two heartbeats she was kissing him back. She had to wonder if she had intentionally provoked him into making another pass, if maybe she'd been waiting all day for this chance. It wasn't a happy thought, but maybe she was a little more deceptive than she cared to admit.

When he broke the kiss for a breath of air and then kissed her again, she stopped thinking entirely. Her heart was pounding, her blood racing, and the heat radiating from each of them would warm her small house on a winter night. Her arms went up around his neck, and his hands slid down her back to cup her buttocks and bring her closer to the fire in his loins.

"Gwen...sweetheart," he whispered raggedly before claiming yet another kiss.

She was totally gone and didn't care. Her kisses had become as hungry as his, her hands every bit as bold. He unbuttoned her blouse and buried his face between her breasts, and she yanked the bottom of his shirt from his jeans and slid her hands up his chest.

For one second they looked into each other's eyes, and what they both wanted was so apparent, no discussion was necessary.

"Your bedroom?" Zane whispered.

"Yes."

He bent slightly, picked her up and carried her from the kitchen. She hugged his neck and pressed kisses to the throbbing pulse beat in his throat. "The room at the end of the hall," she whispered thickly as he strode through the living room.

In her bedroom he let her feet slide to the floor. Shakily she shut the door, and when she turned around he was already undressing. Her breath caught in her throat. He glowed with good looks and vitality. Truly he was the most handsome man she'd ever seen, and deep in her soul she knew that what she was about to do was a result of love. She could never hope for him to love her in the same way, but maybe a woman in her situation had to take any happiness fate handed out, and not worry about tomorrow.

It seemed to be a sensible philosophy, and she quickly began shedding her own clothes. Zane got naked first, and he turned down the bed and lay watching her finish up. The sensuality of his eyes on her while she undressed brought Gwen's desire to a fever pitch, and when she slid down her panties and felt his hot gaze devouring her, she became emotional enough to cry.

Blinking back tears, she crawled into bed and snuggled into his arms. "My darling," he whispered. She soaked up his endearment like a thirsty sponge and started pressing kisses to his chest. Her hand, seemingly of its own accord, went directly to his arousal. She felt driven to touch and caress him intimately, and she could tell how strongly it affected him.

Almost roughly he pushed her onto her back and lay on top of her. His kisses fell all over her face and then his mouth opened on hers. His tongue teased hers until she was moaning, and she opened her legs wider, all but begging for the final act.

"I have protection," he whispered, and reached over the edge of the bed for his wallet.

"Glad you thought of it," she mumbled while he put on a condom. As easily as she got pregnant, *she* should have thought of it.

But she hadn't. Her mind was full of him and the

pleasure he was already giving her, and her body was aching for the rest of it. Aching for those few deliciously explosive moments that ultimately resulted in a sensation of utter peace.

"Zane…oh, Zane," she said hoarsely when he entered her and began moving within her. "It's so good…so good."

"It's better than good, darlin'."

"Yes…better…than good," she moaned. She had never before felt one-tenth of what she was feeling with Zane. Never before had every single cell in her body caught fire, and never before had she wanted and yearned and ached with such desperation.

Try as she might, she could not remain silent. If she woke the kids she would never forgive herself, but the sounds coming from her own throat were unstoppable. Her fingertips dug into Zane's back, and she writhed beneath him, raising and lowering her hips to match his rhythm.

Zane was almost crazed by her response. Never had he made love to a more passionate woman. He'd suspected her ardor because of the theater incident, but to actually feel it, to be the recipient of it, was making him wild. Everything fled his mind but the building pleasure. Every thrust into her feverish body brought him a step closer to the final inferno. It astonished him that she had become almost an extension of his own body. They moved as one; they were a perfect match, a perfect fit.

And to make it even more perfect, they climaxed at exactly the same moment. Stunned and totally sated, he collapsed on her.

Neither of them moved so much as a finger for a very long time.

Eleven

Gwen was so exhausted that when Zane put his arms around her and turned her back to him, she immediately fell asleep. Laying on her side, snuggled with her back to his chest, she didn't know that he tenderly kissed her temple and shoulder, or that he lay there holding her for a long time while he relived the incredible passion they had just shared.

Then he thought of Gwen's kids, and how hard she worked to support them, and that she had sat in the Emergency Room with Ashley for hours and not once complained to anyone. His admiration for her was enormous. He'd never met another woman to compare. Certainly none of the beauties he was accustomed to escorting around town could measure up.

Was he finally falling in love? He frowned. Did he *want* to fall in love?

Uneasily he stretched a leg. Did a man have any say in the matter? Did love just land on a person like a ton of bricks and knock him for a loop, or was it possible to be in love and still maintain control of one's life?

Most people he knew that had fallen in love eventually got married. Were he and Gwen headed for the altar? Was he ready to exchange his free and easy bachelor status for the rank of husband and father? Any man that married a woman with children was at least a stepfather, and if she was a widow, her new husband would be her children's *only* father.

This was a hell of a dilemma, wasn't it? He wanted Gwen more than he'd ever wanted any woman, but did he also want marriage and a ready-made family?

His strength was returning, and holding Gwen's warm naked body was making his own react again. He knew she was tired and he didn't want to wake her, but he couldn't resist running his hand over her smooth skin. Touching her excited him to arousal, and while he tried to keep his breathing at a normal level, even though his heart had sped up, he slowly slid his hand down her belly to that thrilling place between her thighs.

Very gently he moved her legs apart. Closing his eyes then to savor this incredibly sexual moment he started exploring. *Ah, there is nothing like a woman's body.* He loved the feel of her, the uniquely female contours and textures. Though sleeping soundly, she became wet under his fingers, and when he began manipulating the very core of her femininity, she moved against his finger.

Yes, indeed, sweetheart, you are one very hot lady. Her involuntary response pleased him immensely, and it also made *him* hot, much too hot to lie there. Moving cautiously so he wouldn't startle her, he slid his hard, erect member into her from behind.

"My love," he whispered as emotion swelled within him.

Gwen was in the middle of the most fabulous dream. She was being made love to by a man who knew exactly how to pleasure a woman. His hand was right where it should be, stroking, gently stroking, and he filled her again and again with his very hard, very large, positively marvelous manhood.

She whimpered and wriggled in dream-like delight as the thrills compounded. Zane was amazed that she didn't wake up…or was she merely pretending to still be asleep? He stopped moving and waited a few moments to see what she would do, and all she did was sigh as though something precious had just been taken from her.

She was definitely sleeping, and he was so charmed by her that he whispered, ''Maybe I am in love with you, you adorable woman.'' He began moving again, taking it easy, going slow and enjoying every feverish second of this furtive lovemaking. Nothing like this had ever happened to him before; it was a brand-new experience, and he loved it. He wondered, though, if she would wake up before it was over.

But because he was in no hurry, it went on and on, and so did Gwen's wonderful dream. She cried out in her sleep again and again, because she went over the edge again and again, and every time she did it, Zane's adoration of her passionate nature increased.

It was truly the most sensual experience of his life, one against which he knew he would forever measure any other sexual encounter. Finally, he could hold himself back no longer, and he gritted his teeth to keep himself from shouting at the final rush.

Too spent to even leave her body, he shut his eyes and fell asleep.

Gwen opened one eye and saw the nightstand clock. It read 4:10 a.m., and she could feel Zane's leg against hers. He was still here!

Turning over, she sat up, yanked the edge of the sheet around her torso and shook Zane's arm. "Zane."

His eyelids fluttered partially open. "Hi, darlin'. What's going on?"

"It's four in the morning, and I think you should probably go. I don't want my kids seeing you in my bed."

The slight panic in Gwen's voice and eyes made him frown. "Do they usually get up at four?"

"I never know when one of them will come wandering in. I'm surprised it hasn't already happened. Come on, Zane, please get up and go."

"I will...I will," he said with a touch of early morning grouchiness. Then his entire mood changed— she was pretty darn cute in that sheet, with her hair all mussed—and he grinned. "Four is still awfully early. Why don't you move over here and share that sheet with me?"

"No. I shouldn't have done it the first time." Oh, Lord, what nasty little demon had possessed her last night? How could she have been so wanton? She was a respectable, clean-living mother—a widow with morals, for heaven's sake.

Zane's frown deepened as he sensed her regret. "Why not?" he said bluntly.

"We can't talk about this now, Zane, not this morning. There's no time. I don't know what I'd tell my children if they found us naked in bed together. Please go."

"Is it really your kids you're worried about, or yourself? I'm sensing you regret our lovemaking. I don't understand—why is lovemaking so terrible?"

Her patience was wearing a little thin. Why did he have to press the issue right now?

"It seems like you're putting all the blame for last night on me, and that's really not fair."

She faced him squarely. "You're wrong. I wish I *wasn't* one of those fair-minded people and that I *could* say the whole awful mistake was your fault. But I'm blaming myself at least as much as I am you, probably more. But that's an entirely separate issue from the one scaring the daylights out of me now. Really, my kids can't find you here like this."

"Mistake," Zane said softly. "So, it was just a mistake to you." Hurt, he got out of bed and began pulling on his clothes.

Going to the closet, Gwen plucked her bathrobe from a hook on the inside of the door, slipped it on and then let the sheet fall away. Tying the sash around her waist, she turned to check Zane's progress.

He was dressed, sitting on the edge of the bed, putting on his shoes...and watching her. "You're a curious woman," he said. "Why do you think that making love with me was a mistake?"

"Because it was," she said flatly. "It's not going to happen again, Zane, so don't leave this house with any foolish notions." She suddenly had the most discomfiting memory of an embarrassingly erotic dream. But it seemed so real. It *had* been only a dream, hadn't it? She wanted to question him so badly she could hardly keep her mouth shut, but if it *had* been just a dream, talking about it would be utterly humiliating.

Zane laughed softly. From the stunned, almost disoriented expression on her face, he knew that she had remembered their second session of lovemaking. Rather, she was remembering but wondering if she'd dreamed it.

Still worrying about the dream, or whatever it had

been, Gwen moved to the bedroom door. Zane walked over to the door as well, and it never dawned on her that he planned to do anything but leave.

He snaked his arm around her waist and hauled her up against himself. "Zane, don't," she whispered.

"Zane, do," he whispered back. He took hold of the back of her head with his free hand, and then took possession of her lips. It was a lover's kiss—hot, wet and emotional. And Gwen knew at that moment that what had seemed to be a dream was actually the sexiest, most erotic experience of her life.

When he finally stopped kissing her, she couldn't look him in the eye. "I...I'm going to...open the door now," she stammered. "Please don't talk in the hall as we pass the...the children's bedrooms. I really don't want them waking up and seeing you."

"You know it wasn't a dream, don't you?" he said softly.

"Yes, but please don't make me talk about it," she whispered.

He took her chin and tipped up her face. "Gwen, you amaze me. Why does making love embarrass you so much? We're both adults, we're both free agents. And there's something happening between us. Haven't you wondered if it's something important?"

"There's nothing important happening between us, Zane, and there never will be. There's such an enormous chasm between your life and mine that we might as well be from different planets. Now, please be quiet." She opened the door and listened.

With a disgusted shake of his head, Zane followed her into the hall. She said nothing, he said nothing, and neither of them made any other sound.

And yet, there was Donnie, standing in his bedroom doorway, looking sleepy-eyed and curious.

"Hi, Zane," the little boy said. "Mom? Where you going?"

Gwen shot Zane a venomous told-you-so look, then hugged her son and led him back to his bed. "It's too early to get up, sweetheart," she told Donnie as she kissed his smooth little-boy cheek. After tucking the covers around him, she returned to the hall, said not a word to Zane and preceded him to the front door.

"Go," she said.

"Donnie seeing me is not the end of the world," Zane said quietly.

"Please just go," she said wearily.

"Fine. Good night." He walked out.

By nine that morning Gwen had taken her shower and gotten dressed, fed the kids breakfast, and seen to their baths and clothes for the day. She'd arranged a bed on the sofa for Ashley to lie on and tuned the TV to the comical cartoon channel. Since her own activities were going to be confined to the house today because of Ashley, she decided to bake some cookies.

Her doorbell rang at ten. Quickly rinsing her hands at the kitchen sink, she dried them as she went to see who had come calling. *Not Zane. Please, not Zane.*

She opened the door to her parents, and her nervousness turned to glee. "Mom, Dad! Goodness, what a nice surprise." She received two big hugs. "Come in."

Lillian began jabbering as she and Jack went in. "We weren't sure what Sunday School service you brought the kids to, so if you're getting ready to go, just say so."

"We're not going this morning, Mom."

Lillian spied Ashley on the sofa. "What happened?" she cried, and ran over to her little granddaughter.

"I fell off a horse, Grandma," Ashley said proudly. "I have five stitches."

"A horse!" Jack exclaimed. "What in heck were you doing on a horse?"

"I was riding it," Ashley replied, looking a bit startled that she would have to explain something so obvious to a grown-up.

"I rode a horse too, Grandpa," Donnie said, anxious about Grandpa Jack thinking that Ashley might have done something exciting that he hadn't. "I really like horses. I wish we lived on a ranch."

Jack looked at his daughter. "So this horseback riding took place on a ranch?"

Gwen felt like squirming under her father's disapproving gaze, but she managed to smile and say, "Yes. How about some coffee and fresh-baked cookies? Come to the kitchen so we can talk. Kids, I'll bring you some cookies too."

Lillian and Jack took off their lightweight jackets and sat at the kitchen table. Gwen quickly made coffee, then brought a plate of cookies to the living room. "Two apiece," she said firmly to her children. Returning to the kitchen, she prepared another plate with cookies and set it on the table, along with small plates, cups and napkins.

"Goodness, you're a whirlwind this morning," Lillian said. "Come and sit down."

"I had to get things ready, Mom." Gwen pulled out a chair from the table and sat. "The coffee will be done in a few minutes. So,'' she said, looking from one parent to the other, ''how have you two been?''

''We're fine,'' Jack said. ''How have *you* been? Tell us about the ranch and the horses the kids rode. Whose ranch did you visit?''

''Oh, the coffee's done.'' Gwen got up for the pot and filled their cups. Seated again, she cautiously sipped from hers. ''Now, what were we talking about?''

''About the Fortune ranch,'' Jack said sternly.

''Yes,'' Gwen said slowly, realizing that her father had put two and two together. ''It was the Fortune ranch. Something wrong with that, Dad?''

''Maybe. This Zane guy. How's he treating you?''

''Uh, I'm not sure what you're getting at.''

''Don't play games, Gwen. We're not in the Fortunes' class, and just what does Zane Fortune want from you?'' Gwen could feel herself turn three shades of red. ''Aha! I knew he was up to no good. Lil, didn't I tell you?''

''Now, Jack,'' Lillian admonished. ''Don't jump to any hasty conclusions. Gwen, um, has Zane Fortune become a good friend? He would be an incredible catch for a woman in your situation.''

''Mom!'' Gwen exclaimed, appalled that her mother was hearing wedding bells simply because Zane was wealthy. ''I have absolutely no unrealistic hopes where Zane is concerned. He's one of Help-Mate's clients, which is how we met. And yes, I've seen him a few times beyond the work I do for him. But—''

''So we understand your hopes. What about his?''

Gwen was on a very hot seat. In the first place, she didn't know any more about Zane's hopes where she was concerned than her father did. Or, in all honesty, if Zane even had any. Last night he'd gotten what she had believed all along that he'd been wanting from her, and maybe that's all there would ever be to their relationship.

"I have no idea what Zane Fortune thinks about anything," she said flatly, and lifted her cup for a swallow of coffee, meeting her father's stern, disapproving eyes over the rim. Lowering the cup she added, "And that is the end of this discussion. I'm very happy to see each of you, but I'm not going to talk any further about Zane."

"You're not telling us something," Jack accused.

"Oh, Dad, I haven't told you everything since I was sixteen years old, maybe even before that."

"Well, you won't think it's so cute when it's your kids keeping things from you."

"I'm sure you're right," Gwen said quietly. She picked up the plate of cookies and held them toward her father. "Have a cookie, Dad, and let's talk about something else. You've always been wonderful parents, especially since Paul died. I have a little money in the bank, and I'm going to make a payment on what I owe you. Wait here."

Rushing from the kitchen to her bedroom, Gwen grabbed her checkbook and hurried back. She sat again and wrote a check for three hundred dollars, which she handed to her father.

He looked at the amount, then at her. "How can you afford this?"

She hadn't expected the question and she started stammering. "I...I..."

"Did Zane Fortune give you money?" Jack was glowering.

"Uh...yes, but I, uh, earned it." *Oh my God, what*

*if he asks how I earned it? I could never confess that
I took money from Zane to lie to his family. Mom and
Dad would be devastated by such behavior.*

Scowling, Jack got to his feet. "Lillian, it's time we
left."

"But we just got here, honey."

Gwen knew she should plead with her father to stay
longer, but she couldn't force the words out of her
mouth. Jack Lafferty's mind was not easily changed
once set on something, and it was obvious that he
didn't like his daughter's association with Zane Fortune one little bit. If she did get him to stay longer,
she knew it was all he would talk about. He might
even say things she would not be able to forgive.

So it was with a genuine but sad relief that she saw
her parents to the door and kissed them goodbye.

Returning to the kitchen she sat at the table again,
and her gaze fell on her checkbook. She was spending
the two-thousand, and if Zane ever did tell her how
much the repairs to his car had cost she probably
wouldn't have the money to reimburse him.

"To heck with it," she mumbled. He should have
told her right away.

Her eyes watered with unshed tears. There were a
lot of things Zane should have done, a lot he shouldn't
have, but none of his sins compared to the stupidity
of hers. Even though no battle lines had ever been
drawn between them, he'd won the first skirmish of a
very emotional war of wills. At least it was emotional
for her. She could only guess at his feelings.

At any rate, she'd made a complete fool of herself
with Zane last night, and she hadn't done much better
with her parents today.

Gwen put her face in her hands and groaned, doing
so quietly to keep her misery private from her children. Maybe she deserved to suffer, but they didn't.

Twelve

Later that afternoon Gwen had a long telephone conversation with Ramona, explaining how Ashley had gotten injured and about the ordeal of the Emergency Room. Ramona listened with few questions, but then finally said, "He's gorgeous, Gwen."

"Who is?"

"Do you have the gall to act like you don't know to whom I'm referring? Zane, Gwen—Zane Fortune. He is so good-looking that I would have liked to just stand there on my own front porch last night and stare at him. Thank goodness I didn't."

Gwen sighed. "Yes, he's good-looking."

Ramona was silent a moment, then asked quietly, "What's wrong, Gwen?"

"Nothing," Gwen said quickly. She was afraid of saying too much about Zane; she really couldn't tell anyone about last night, not even her best friend. "Nothing more than the usual, that is. Um, Mom and Dad dropped in this morning."

It was a good change of subject, even though it could have led to Zane too, if Gwen had let it. Instead she and Ramona discussed their respective parents for a while and finally said goodbye. Gwen hung up and eyed the phone. She'd seen her parents and talked to Ramona today. There was no one else she wanted to hear from.

Switching on the answering machines, she walked into the living room, saw that Mindy was falling asleep on the floor next to the sofa, and picked up the tot. "Time for your nap, little darling," she whispered as she carried Mindy to her crib.

After checking Ashley again and finding no sign of fever, Gwen decided to work on the old furniture in her garage. She told the kids where she would be and not to answer the phone. "Let the machine pick up any messages, okay?"

"Okay, Mom," they both agreed.

Gwen was still moving furniture around, undecided about which piece to work on, when her mother walked in through the connecting door between the house and garage. Obviously Donnie had let her in.

"Mom! For goodness' sake, two visits in one day?" Panic suddenly seized Gwen. "Is Dad all right?"

"Your father is fit to be tied, but that's all that's wrong with him," Lillian said dryly. "Anyway, he sent me over here to return this." She pulled Gwen's check from her purse and put it in her daughter's hand.

"Return it!" Gwen exclaimed, completely baffled. "Why, for heaven's sake? I owe you a lot more than this."

"Because it came from Zane Fortune." Lillian held up her hand. "Now don't go getting mad at me about this. I'm merely the go-between."

Gwen couldn't help getting angry. "That's the silliest thing I've ever heard! What's wrong with Zane's money?"

"Gwen, you know your father. He's got it in his mind that Zane is taking advantage of you. Actually, we've been arguing about it since we left here this morning. I told him that you've never let anyone take advantage of you, but Jack's the most stubborn, mule-headed—''

''Mom, no,'' Gwen said hastily. Her parents had always had a wonderful relationship, a good marriage, and the thought of them arguing over her and Zane was horrifying. ''If it makes Dad feel better, I'll tear up the check. But please don't fight because of me.''

Donnie came running in. ''Can I have another cookie, Mom? Ashley wants one too.''

Lillian caught her grandson and hugged him. ''Do you want to get fat?'' she teased.

''You should've seen how much I ate at Zane's ranch,'' Donnie boasted.

''Did you really? You must have had good food,'' Lillian remarked while looking at her daughter.

''Yeah, it was real good,'' Donnie said.

Even though Gwen was looking pained, Lillian asked, ''Donnie, do you like Mr. Fortune?''

Donnie shrugged and said, ''Guess so.'' He looked at his mother. ''Mom, what time was it when I saw Zane in the night?''

Gwen's jaw dropped. So did Lillian's. ''Go ahead and get your sister and yourself a cookie,'' Gwen mumbled to her son.

''Yeah, but what time—?'' Donnie persisted.

''Never mind, it doesn't matter.'' Donnie ran out, and Gwen and her mother stood like two statues staring at each other.

''He stayed the night, didn't he,'' Lillian finally said, almost sadly. ''Gwen, are you in love with him?''

Gwen looked away. ''Please don't ask me that.''

''Are you unsure of yourself, or of him?''

Gwen thought a moment, then sighed. ''Circumstance is the real problem, Mom. Look who he is, and then take a look at who I am.''

''Are you telling me that you would be in love with him if he weren't a Fortune? Gwen, if you believe that, you're deluding yourself. Either you're in love or you're not, and the same goes for him with you.'' Lillian's expression became seriously thoughtful. ''Have the two of you talked about feelings? And 'circumstance,' as you put it?''

''Mom, I really don't want to discuss Zane. I'm just not in the mood.'' Gwen stepped over to an old library table that was layered with decades of dirt. ''Help me make a decision. Should I work on this piece or that chest of drawers over there?''

''The table,'' Lillian said absently. ''Gwen, do you realize what marrying into the Fortune family would do for you?'

''Mom!'' Gwen gasped. ''I hope you don't think I would ever marry a man for his money.''

''Oh, for heaven's sake, Zane's not some old geezer you could barely stand to have touch you. Obviously you're attracted to him or you wouldn't have let him stay with you last night.''

''I do not believe what I'm hearing. My own mother, the soul of propriety, actually suggesting I go after a man for his money.'' Gwen shook her head and added, ''Tell me you were only kidding, Mom.''

Lillian hesitated a few moments, then said, ''Answer me this, Gwen. What are Zane's intentions toward you?''

Gwen smiled wryly. ''Well, he's certainly not after my money.''

''You do know about his reputation with women.''

"Yes, Mom, I do. Everyone in San Antonio knows about it."

"Has it occurred to you that fooling around with Zane could make you the talk of the town?"

Gwen shrugged. "Who cares? The gossip would only last as long as the relationship."

"Aha! You just admitted there *is* a relationship." Lillian sidled toward the door. "I'm going to leave now and let you get to work. I'll call this evening to find out how Ashley is doing. And you might phone your father and me a little more often. We worry about you, whether you want us to or not."

Gwen let that comment pass and smiled. "Talk to you later, Mom."

"'Bye, honey."

After Lillian had gone, Gwen sank onto a dusty old chair to fret. *Surely Mom wasn't serious. But maybe she was. It would be a ton of worry off her and Dad's minds if I ever became financially secure.*

Gwen realized that her body had become quite tense. She felt as though powerful pressures and conflicting opinions were pulling at her, tugging her first one way and then another.

She covered her eyes with her hands, groaned quietly and wished again that she'd never met Zane. Now her parents knew just enough to worry themselves sick, and wasn't she herself in just about the same boat? After all, what did she know about Zane's feelings, other than the obvious?

And maybe last night had even satisfied the "obvious"—his lust for her.

A chill went up Gwen's spine over that thought, but she couldn't deny the possibility. In fact, the more she thought about it, the more probable it seemed. She'd

been an awful fool last night, and if her mother had
gone home with a hope that something permanent was
going to come out of her daughter's and Zane Fortune's relationship, then Lillian was in for a rude
awakening.

"Just forget Zane," Gwen whispered unsteadily.
"You have to forget him."

It was good advice, but could she heed it when her
heart felt broken in a zillion pieces because she knew,
she *knew,* there was no future for her and Zane?

Zane's first Monday at the office after Thanksgiving
was swamped. Even though he was almost frenetically
busy, personal thoughts kept sneaking up on him. After unforgettable lovemaking, Gwen had unceremoniously kicked him out of her bed and house. He hadn't
taken it well, and, in fact, had sworn to stay away from
her. They hadn't spoken since that night one week
ago. He refused to call her, and she hadn't called him.
But now he accused himself of adolescent sensitivity.
What he should have done was go back to Gwen's
house that very day and check her mood, or at least
phone her. Instead—and it bothered him that he could
behave so childishly—he'd hung around his own
house, sulked, and told himself that no woman walked
on Zane Fortune and got away with it.

Now, of course, the whole incident had compounded into a *situation.* He'd told himself repeatedly
during the past week that Gwen could have called him
as easily as he could have called her, but that argument
simply didn't fly. Gwen would never call him. If he
was ever going to see her again, it was up to him. It
was as simple as that.

Or…as complex.

Around two that afternoon Heather gave a quick *rap* on Zane's door and stepped into his office. "There's a Jack Lafferty parked on the chair next to my desk. He didn't ask to see you, Zane. He announced rather fiercely that he *had* to see you. Zane, he's Gwen Hutton's father, or so he said, but do you know him? He seems very upset, and well, I was wondering if I should call security. To tell you the truth, I don't know how he got clear up here when he's so obviously angry. Someone should have noticed and stopped him from getting into an elevator. Isn't that why the first floor is crawling with security people?"

Zane's brow furrowed. "Gwen's father? And he wants to see me?"

"Not 'wants,' 'has to,' according to him," Heather replied. She bit her lip a moment, then said thoughtfully, "Why on earth would Gwen's father come here in such a foul mood?"

Zane had a few disturbing ideas about that, but he kept them to himself and got to his feet. "I'll see him. Please show him in, Heather."

"Are you sure?" Clearly, Heather was concerned.

"Yes, I'm sure." Heather left, and Zane began moving papers and file folders around on his desk so it wouldn't look so cluttered. Zane realized that in a way he really did want to meet Gwen's father. Her mother too, someday. Besides, if Jack Lafferty had come here angry, it had something to do with Gwen. Zane had no idea how much Jack might know about the powerful attraction between him and Gwen, but Zane knew he would be stupid not to see her father, shake his hand and make friends with him.

The office door opened again and Heather preceded a huge bear of a man with graying dark hair and shoulders a yard wide into the room. He was wearing jeans, boots, a plaid cotton shirt and a denim jacket, and he looked muscular and hard as nails. He wasn't smiling.

"Mr. Lafferty," Heather said, "this is Zane Fortune. Zane, Jack Lafferty. Will there be anything else before I leave you two alone?"

Zane smiled at Jack, then spoke to Heather, who seemed to be sending warning signals with her eyes. "Not unless Jack would like something to drink. How about a cup of coffee? Or a soda, Jack?"

"Nothing," Jack said flatly, still with no sign of a smile.

Zane rounded his desk with his right hand extended. "It's good to meet Gwen's father."

Jack shook Zane's hand, but he all but snarled, "You might not think meeting me's so great before I leave this fancy office, Fortune."

Zane realized then just how ticked off and belligerent Jack Lafferty really was. Gwen's father had definitely come here with a chip on his shoulder. Since they had no common ground but Gwen, she must be behind Jack's anger. Exactly in what way Zane didn't know, but he figured he would soon find out.

"Have a seat," Zane said quietly, and sat on his own chair behind his desk.

"I'd just as soon stand," Jack said, putting his huge hands on the back of a chair and glaring across Zane's desk at him. "I'm here because of Gwen."

"Figured you were, but don't expect me to get into any kind of personal conversation about her. I don't happen to talk to other people about the women I know—not even with their fathers." After a second Zane added, "Maybe especially their fathers."

"Oh, you'll discuss my daughter, if I have to hold

you down and sit on you." Jack Lafferty's snapping black eyes just dared Zane to defy him. "You stayed at her house Saturday night, a week ago. My anger over that has been building, Fortune, and now I'm asking—exactly how long has that been going on?"

Obviously Donnie had spilled the beans. He couldn't imagine Gwen herself telling her father how far things had gone between them that night. It was Donnie, he told himself, probably innocently saying something about having seen Zane in the middle of the night.

"You know, Jack," Zane said calmly, "that's really none of your business. But just to keep things friendly, I'll tell you one thing. That night was a first."

Jack's eyes narrowed dangerously. "Was it also a last?"

It took Zane a second to get his meaning. "You're asking if it was a one-night stand? Is that what you think of your daughter?"

"I love my daughter, you rich, spoiled *Fortune!*" Jack shouted. "And she doesn't need the likes of you turning her into a...a..."

"A what, Jack?" Zane asked in a chilly voice as he got to his feet, all but daring Jack to go too far. He felt like calling security himself and having Jack Lafferty thrown out on his ear. If he hadn't been Gwen's dad, Zane just might have done it too.

Jack's face reddened. "You just be careful, buster. You're talking about my daughter."

"And you're being totally irrational. Please, sit down and cool off." Zane followed his own advice and resumed sitting in his chair. He was relieved when Jack finally sat too, even though Jack put on a big show of reluctance and shot several threatening looks at Zane.

Zane waited for Jack to say something, and when he didn't, Zane said, "For your information, I have the utmost respect for Gwen."

That comment unleashed Lafferty's tongue, and he growled, "From where I sit it looks like you're taking advantage of her. She's alone—except for her kids—and probably lonely a lot of the time. Someone like you probably looks pretty good to her."

Zane cocked an eyebrow. "Someone like me?"

"Yeah, someone like you," Jack said belligerently. "Make anything you want out of that, but let me tell you something, buster, I want your affair with my daughter to come to a halt here and now. In fact, I want your word on it."

"My word!" Zane snorted. "Listen, Lafferty, if Gwen and I stop seeing each other, it will be our decision, not yours."

"Is that so?" Jack snarled. "Okay, answer me this, and it's a question I have every right to ask. What kind of intentions do you have toward Gwen? I'm not talking about how she might be feeling about you, Fortune, I'm talking about your feelings for her. Is she just another short-term bed partner or does she mean something to you?"

"She means a great deal to me." Zane was a little surprised at his quick answer, and couldn't help wondering if he was letting Jack Lafferty intimidate him.

"And?" Jack said, pressing for more. Zane just sat there, and Jack got to his feet. Putting his palms on the desk, he leaned over it. *"And?"* he demanded hotly.

"I'd like to marry her...if she'll have me," Zane blurted.

Jack straightened his back and smiled. "Stand up and shake your future father-in-law's hand, son."

Before Jack left Zane's office, Zane made him promise to say nothing to Gwen about this discussion until he could actually propose—which he knew wasn't going to be simple when they hadn't even talked in over a week. But Jack readily agreed and walked out with a huge grin on his face.

It was then that Zane's knees got weak, and he practically collapsed into his chair with a stunned expression on his face. He could hardly believe what he'd just done, and there'd been no good reason for it. He could have gotten rid of Jack Lafferty with the push of a button.

But something had stopped him from alienating Gwen's father and causing a rift that might never heal. The thing was, if he didn't really plan on marrying Gwen, what difference would it have made if Jack had been tossed out with him cursing every Fortune who'd ever been born?

To Zane, marriage had always seemed the most monumental step in a man's life, and he had never been sure that he wanted to get married. What made this all so crazy, though, was that he couldn't stop thinking about Gwen when he knew darn well that he was treading on thin ice with her. She was not a love 'em-and-leave 'em type of woman, and he knew in his soul that if he wanted to protect and maintain his bachelor status he should stay completely away from her.

Despite that indelible knowledge, Zane could not get Gwen out of his mind. He crudely asked himself if one reason she was so unforgettable was that she was so much better in bed than any other woman he'd made love with—and shocked himself with a "Yes!" answer.

But then, that told him he wasn't thinking with his brain where Gwen was concerned, which made the affair all that more dangerous. Actually, it was a pretty volatile situation all around, considering that Gwen's dad believed that Zane intended to propose.

For days after his conversation with Jack, Zane kept wondering if Gwen's father would keep his word about saying nothing to Gwen about their conversation. By Thursday he could no longer argue himself out of attempting to talk to her to find out what she did or didn't know. He dialed her home number and was surprised when she answered. He was tired of getting one of those cursed machines of hers.

"Hello, Gwen," he said in a cheerful, upbeat voice, as though there never had been any animosity between them. "How are you?"

The rippling response Gwen felt throughout her system at the sound of Zane's voice instantly put her on guard. "I'm okay," she said distantly, and deliberately did not ask how he was.

Zane ignored her frosty tone and forged on. "How about the kids? How's Ashley doing?"

"She's fine, they're all fine." Gwen couldn't resist asking, "Are you really interested in my kids, or are you merely being polite?"

"You're still upset with me. I'm not sure what I'm apologizing for, but I'm sorry. Actually, I'm surprised to find myself talking to you at all. I thought I'd get your answering machine."

"It quit working and I haven't been able to fix it. Guess I'm going to have to replace it with a new one.

The one connected to my business number still works, but the other one gave up the ghost.''

Zane realized that she did not remotely sound like a woman expecting a marriage proposal, and he breathed a sigh of relief. Apparently Jack was a man of his word.

That feeling was reinforced when Gwen asked, ''Is there a reason for this call? I was just putting the kids to bed.''

''Um, yeah, a good reason,'' Zane said before he thought about it. ''How about dinner together tomorrow night?''

''You're asking me out again?'' Gwen sounded as incredulous as she felt. For almost two weeks she'd heard nothing from him, and she'd been recovering— at least a little—from his influence. The last thing she wanted was to start at square one again with Zane, and she might as well let him know how she felt about that.

''That's the idea, yes,'' he said with a small chuckle.

She wasn't amused. ''No,'' she said flatly. ''And this time I mean it, Zane. Don't ask me out again. We are *not* going to have a long-term affair, or even a two-or three-week affair. Please don't call me again.'' She slammed down the phone.

Zane was caught completely off guard. With the line dead, he finally put down the phone and then stared at it broodingly.

Jack Lafferty thought Zane was going to propose to his daughter, and Gwen had absolutely no affection for him. What a peculiar turn of events this was!

Thirteen

During the following days Gwen worked harder than ever. Whenever time and her Help-Mate schedule permitted, she worked on the old furniture in her garage. Physically she rarely stopped moving, and at night she went to bed tired and ready for sleep.

But no matter how busy she kept herself, and how much she exhausted her body so she would sleep at night, her mind still played dirty tricks on her. When she least expected it, Zane and a dozen disturbing memories would suddenly invade her brain. As unnerved as those invasions made her feel, there didn't seem to be anything she could do to stop the onslaughts. She suffered them in tense, teary-eyed silence, while wishing with every fiber of her being that she'd said no to everything Zane had ever suggested, from their very first meeting.

And then, on occasion, she found herself balking and thinking some very strange thoughts. One was about just saying to hell with every standard she'd ever lived by and phoning Zane and telling him that she would gladly have any kind of affair with him that he could name. She actually trembled every time that idea passed through her mind, because it was truly earth-shaking. She had three children for whom she must keep up appearances, after all, and two moralistic, watchful parents, who, incidentally, had started calling her so much that it was becoming annoying.

One particular phone call stood out. She and her mother had been talking about nothing in particular when suddenly her mother blurted, "Don't you have something to tell us, honey?"

Gwen thought hard. Had she missed relating some little incident about the kids? It occurred to her then that she'd talked to her folks so often during the last few weeks that they even knew what she'd been feeding the kids for meals!

"Mom, there is nothing I haven't told you and Dad. What are you hoping to hear?"

"Hmm," Lillian said thoughtfully.

"Hmm, what?" Gwen demanded. "Mom, what's going on?"

"Not a thing, dear. I'll call again later. 'Bye."

Gwen had hung up muttering that she *had* to take enough time from work to shop for a new answering machine. At least then she would be able to screen some of these completely senseless calls. Not that she resented talking to her parents. But they were both acting so oddly, almost as if they knew some sort of secret and were just waiting for her to find it out. If they knew something that she should know, why wouldn't they just come right out and tell her about it?

And so one day followed another and Gwen did her best not to dwell on the fact that her life as it was now was probably all it would ever be. She had no faith whatsoever in meeting the "perfect" man—the only thing that might change her life-style—because, first of all, no one was perfect, and, second, a woman with three kids and no money of her own was about as much in demand among single men as a case of the mumps.

Not that she couldn't indulge in affairs, if she so decided. Both she and Ramona could have had bed partners almost from the day their husbands had died. And maybe it was naive to hope to fall in love again someday, but it was how they both felt.

The painful thing, of course, was that Gwen *had* fallen in love...with a man she couldn't even envision as a husband—hers or any other woman's. No, as sad as it was, she could not see Zane as a married man, even though she had to admit that he'd surprised her with his response to the kids the day of the barbecue. But his being nice to five little kids for one day guaranteed nothing. It certainly didn't make him less predatory or any more domesticated than she knew him to be.

He was a dyed-in-the-wool bachelor, and for her own good she'd best keep that in mind.

Zane had never come up against a problem of this nature before, and he couldn't seem to reach any kind of satisfactory solution to it. Completely eliminating Gwen from his life would solve everything, of course, but whenever he reached that conclusion he felt an intolerable ache in his gut, and he would quickly switch his thoughts to other possibilities.

The thing that bothered him most was that unspoken marriage proposal hanging over his head. What on earth had possessed him to say such a thing to Gwen's father? And there was one other thing. When Zane had asked Jack not to mention it to Gwen until he could, Jack had readily agreed. But time was passing, and Jack Lafferty didn't strike Zane as a patient man. In fact, Zane half expected the older man to come barreling back into his office any day yelling, "Hey, buster, let's get this show on the road!"

It really was the most absurd situation of Zane's life, and he had to wonder about his own part in it. He hated the possibility that he'd let Jack Lafferty's angry bluster intimidate him into saying something he would never have said without prodding. But since he couldn't remember another occasion on which someone had intimidated him, that explanation for what he'd blurted out to Lafferty seemed pretty lame.

And yet he'd said it. He couldn't deny saying it, nor could he pretend that Lafferty hadn't taken him seriously.

What he had to do, he finally decided, was talk to Gwen. He had to tell her the whole story, keep it light and hope she thought it was funny. It would be disappointing if she got mad instead, but why would she? And even if she didn't see the incident as funny, wouldn't any anger she felt be aimed at her dad and not at Zane?

It amazed Zane how much he didn't want Gwen mad at him. He'd have to get past her anger from their last conversation somehow, and then convince her to see him long enough to have a discussion. Surely he was smart enough to figure out a way to accomplish that.

Eventually an idea gelled. About a week after Gwen hung up on him, Zane stopped at Heather's desk on his way into his own office.

"Good morning, Zane," she said.

"Morning," he replied with a deliberately reflective expression, a *serious* expression, as though a dilemma of great consequence was on his mind.

"Is something wrong?" Heather asked.

"Well...I suppose there is," Zane said slowly. "I've been trying to speak to Gwen Hutton for days without any luck. She's an expert at refinishing furniture, and I have several pieces..." Zane paused briefly. "That wouldn't matter, except that I'm planning a big party over the Christmas holidays and would like everything in the house to be perfect."

"Oh," Heather murmured, sounding as though she'd expected to hear something of importance, and his trivial little problem really didn't deserve the long face he was wearing.

Realizing that he was laying it on a bit thick, Zane grinned. "Anyhow, since Gwen is obviously unimpressed with my attempts to speak to her and won't return my calls, I'd like you to make contact with her and give her a message for me."

"I'll certainly try," Heather said, and picked up a pen. "What is the message?"

"I would like her to meet me at my home at four this afternoon so I can show her the pieces that need refinishing. We'll discuss the particulars at that time, and the whole thing shouldn't take more than twenty, thirty minutes. It's important that you stress the fact that I do not intend to take up much of her time. Uh, tell her that I have a five o'clock business appointment."

Heather looked up from her pad with a startled expression. "I don't have anything for five in your appointment book. How did I miss—"

"You didn't. This just came up, and it—it's, uh, only partially business. Nothing to concern yourself about, Heather." Zane glanced at his watch. "I'd better get to work. Please try to reach Gwen right away, and if you don't succeed, please keep trying."

"Yes, I'll do that."

Zane felt his secretary's curiosity-filled eyes on his back all the way to his office door. Going in, he shut the door behind himself and sighed. Why *wouldn't* Heather be curious? She'd worked for him long enough to know that when a piece of furniture in his house started showing signs of wear, he replaced it. Since he wasn't into antiques, collectibles or priceless originals, everything in his house was easily replaceable.

But he'd racked his brain for a logical excuse for Heather to spend most of the day trying to get hold of Gwen for him, and the furniture idea had seemed best.

Now, he thought while seating himself at his desk, all he had to do was wait for Heather to tell him that she had talked to Gwen and the four o'clock appointment at his house was fine.

He was positive Heather would succeed where he had failed.

When Gwen checked Help-Mate's answering machine around ten that morning and heard that Heather needed to speak to her, she phoned at once.

"This is Gwen Hutton, Heather. What's up?"

"Oh, Gwen. Thanks for calling back so quickly. I have a message from Zane for you. Apparently he has some furniture that needs refinishing. He would like you to meet him at his house at four this afternoon so he can show you which pieces and also to discuss the particulars. I assume that means price and timing and such. At any rate, he has a busy schedule this afternoon and can only give you about twenty or thirty minutes to go over the work. May I tell him you'll be there?''

Gwen was flabbergasted. In spite of her little garage business, she was far from being an expert on the fine art of putting new finishes on furniture. And, every single thing in Zane's gorgeous house had to have been outrageously expensive. Why on earth would he trust her with his costly things?

"Heather, I really don't…um, understand," she finally stammered.

"You don't understand what?"

While Heather said those four words, two others flashed through Gwen's mind: *Christmas money!*

Hastily she backtracked. "Uh, forget it. Tell Zane I'll meet him at four."

"Good."

"Heather, you're sure he said only twenty or thirty minutes?"

"Positive. He has a five o'clock business meeting."

"Fine. Thanks for the call." Gwen hung up, worried some about destroying instead of improving Zane's excellent furniture, then worried a little about going to his home at all. But she thought again about Christmas, and how great it would be to have some extra money to spend on her kids. She daydreamed about a lovely Christmas for a while, then switched gears again. She had already damaged Zane's car; the thought of ruining some of his furniture gave her cold chills.

Okay, here's what you'll do. After you see what furniture he wants refinished, if you think you can handle it, you'll take the job. Otherwise, you'll tell him no, that he should hire a professional. Since he has a five o'clock appointment, you won't be at his house for

*long and he's not apt to try anything funny. Just play
it cool and keep things impersonal.*

Regardless of all that common sense, Gwen
couldn't help being on edge the rest of the day. It
angered her that almost every one of her daily deci-
sions, both the big ones and the small ones, were influenced by money. In her heart she knew she should
not be going to Zane's house when he was there, but
she needed money for Christmas, and so she had to
ignore her heart's warnings. She had to ignore the
weakness she had for Zane. She had to forget the feelings she kept trying to bury so deeply that they would
never surface again, and the memories she would be
so much better off not having. She had to drive up to
his house and go inside, talk business with him, and
act as though nothing personal had ever passed between them. If he could do it—and she believed he
could, considering his almost ruthless reputation with
women—then so could she.

That was the thought she clung to during the drive
to his house that afternoon. *If he can do it, so can I.*
Though she couldn't help wincing when she saw his
vehicle on the circular driveway, she forced herself to
park her van right behind it instead of going round
back, where she usually parked. Then she got out,
bravely walked to the front door and rang the bell.

She had not changed clothes purposely or done anything special to her hair or makeup. She was not there
for anything but business, and something as simple as
fresh lipstick just might make Zane think otherwise. It
was an awful feeling not to trust herself, but if Zane
did try something, she was honestly afraid she couldn't
say no.

Taking in a huge breath of air so she would appear

calm and collected when he opened the door, she pushed the doorbell again. She could faintly hear the elegant chimes from inside the house, and wondered, a bit impatiently, what was taking Zane so long to come to the door.

In fact, Zane had come to the door, then had been almost paralyzed by complete and utter confusion. He was standing in the foyer wondering how on earth he was going to talk to Gwen about such a delicate matter without destroying any chance they had. *Gwen—ha,ha—I told your dad I was going to propose marriage, but I don't know why I said that and—ha,ha—isn't it just about the funniest thing you've ever heard?*

There was nothing funny about it, and Zane was furious with himself for even hoping that Gwen would laugh. He sure as hell wasn't laughing. He felt like a total jerk, in fact. Getting Gwen to come here with lies was unforgivable.

You had no choice. She wouldn't talk to you on the phone.

That, at least, was the truth, which eased some of Zane's tension. Putting on a more relaxed face, he opened the door. "Hi. Thanks for coming."

"You're welcome." Gwen stepped into the foyer, and Zane closed the door. The second she saw him she felt hot and achy in places where she shouldn't be feeling anything. Not only that, but her mind went into overdrive and dredged up again every detail of their incredible lovemaking. It was not the most propitious start for a business meeting.

She cleared her throat. "Which room contains the pieces you were thinking of having redone?"

"The pool room." That ludicrous answer had come out of nowhere.

"The pool room?" Gwen echoed in surprise. "The *swimming* pool room?"

"Uh, yeah, I moved some things into it." Zane was thinking clearly again, and as hard as it had been to get Gwen here alone, he wasn't going to let her leave without *some* conversation. "It's locked," he told her. "We'll go through the kitchen, and I'll get the key."

"Fine," she agreed, and followed him unquestioningly.

But once inside the pool room, she became *very* questioning, because he locked the door behind them and then tucked the key into his pants pocket.

"What're you doing?" she demanded. "Why did you lock the door?" She glanced around. "And where's the furniture you want refinished?"

Zane leaned his back against the door. "There is no furniture. I mean, there's none that I want refinished. You're here so we can talk."

Gwen's eyes narrowed menacingly. "You had Heather lie to get me here?"

"No, I lied to Heather to get you here. Let me remind you that I would not have had to resort to such a drastic measure if you hadn't slammed the phone down in my ear."

"Then of course your lies and my being here is all my fault." Her voice rose. "Is there anything you wouldn't do to satisfy a whim? You may be a Fortune, but that doesn't give you the right to control or manipulate my life. Unlock that door and let me out of here."

"Sorry, but I can't do that."

"If you dare to stand there and act calm and—and like everything is just peachy...when I'm ready to explode over your deceit, I swear I'll…I'll…" Gwen stopped sputtering, because what could she do?

She walked over to the diving board and sat down. "You know, this could be construed as kidnapping," she said with fire in her eyes. If he got near the edge of the pool, she was going to knock him into the water. He at least deserved to get wet for this fiasco, and if he dunked her in retaliation, so be it, but she really believed that she was fast enough on her feet to stay out of his reach. "And don't think I won't find out for sure and file charges if it is, because the minute I leave here I'm driving straight to the nearest police station."

"You'd have me arrested?"

"In a New York minute."

Zane rubbed his jaw thoughtfully. "Hmm. Can't say I'd like to go to jail just for stealing a few minutes of your time." He took the key from his pocket. "Okay, you can leave. Here's the key. Catch!" He tossed it at her.

Gwen leaped up and tried to catch it but she missed, and it fell in the water. "Look what you've done!" she screeched. "Now it's at the bottom of the pool."

Zane walked to the edge of the pool, hunkered down and peered into the water. "Yep, you're right. There it is."

"You knew I wouldn't catch it! You did that on purpose!"

"I did not," Zane said, sounding boyishly hurt that she would accuse him of something so sneaky.

"You big phony," she seethed, and realized that he was still very close to the pool's edge and practically on his knees. Rushing forward with her hands extended, she hit him hard and he tumbled headfirst into the pool. Only he didn't go alone. How he did it she would never know, but one of his hands closed around her ankle and she went sailing into the water along with him.

She came up sputtering. "Just wait till I get out of here. You are in big trouble."

His response was to dive beneath the water, take her by the legs and pull her under. Again she came up sputtering and yelling, and again he pulled her down, this time clear to the bottom of the pool. She was so shocked she didn't even attempt to find the key. When she came up she coughed and said, "If you're trying to drown me, I'm almost there. And this water's cold too. Are you too cheap to run the heater?"

He swam over to her, and she took a swing at him. He ducked and laughed. "You must want another dunking."

"I want to get out of this—this pool, you miserable man!" she shrieked. "I really am going to have you arrested, you can count on it!"

"You sure are cute all wet. Course, I noticed that the first day we met. Your wet T-shirt was just about the sexiest thing I'd ever seen. The one you're wearing right now is pretty sexy too."

Gwen looked down at her chest and groaned. Her breasts were clearly delineated, her nipples hard and erect. "It's only the cold water," she said furiously, "so don't go getting all macho and think I'm responding to your caveman tactics."

"You're right, the water is cold. I'll have to turn up the heater. But for now I think a sauna is in order—we both need to warm up."

"If you think I'm getting into the sauna with you, think again!" Gwen shrieked.

"I guess I can't force you to get warm, but the sauna's where I'm heading." He took a dive to the bottom of the pool and brought up the key. Grinning at her, he held it up to show her, then swam to the shallow end, where he stood and walked to the steps. "You know where the sauna is, if you change your mind," he called.

"Not a chance," she muttered, then stared in dismay as he got rid of his dripping clothes right in front of her. "Don't you have even one gram of modesty?" she yelled.

"Honey, you've not only seen me naked, you enjoyed every second we *both spent* naked."

"I did not!"

Laughing, he went to a cupboard, took out an enormous pile of folded towels, and carried all of them with him as he disappeared through a door that she knew led to his sauna.

"You rotten manipulator," she whispered. "You took every towel!" Dammit, enough was enough! He could have left her a couple of towels, at least, even if she couldn't escape the pool room.

Enraged, she swam to the shallow end of the pool and climbed up the steps. Her soaked clothes felt like they weighed a ton, and she couldn't stop shivering. But she was mad as hell, so she marched militantly to the sauna door and yanked it open. Zane was stretched out full length on a bench, stark naked, and the big stack of towels was near his head.

"Close the door, you're letting the heat escape," he said while slowly sitting up.

"I want a towel!" She pulled the door shut and the heat of the sauna felt incredible.

"You can have all the towels you want...if you get out of those clothes."

"So you can do what?"

"Not one thing you don't want. Gwen, you have my word. I just don't want you coming down with pneumonia. Think of your kids, if you got sick."

"Yeah, I'm sure that's what *you're* thinking of," she drawled sarcastically. "And your word isn't worth two cents, so save your breath."

"Okay, fine, have it your way." Zane lay down again. "This really feels great. I'm warm all the way through."

She was beginning to get warm, but her sodden clothes still felt awful.

"Are you going to give me the key so I can leave?" she asked while averting her eyes from his nude body.

"Nope."

"I'm never going to forgive you for this, you know."

"Sure you will. Just as soon as you unbend enough to get out of those wet clothes and relax enough for us to do some talking."

She narrowed her eyes suspiciously. "And talking is all you want from me?"

"That's right."

"Do you promise not to do anything but talk?"

"You said my word wasn't worth two cents."

"Do you promise?" she shrieked.

"Okay, okay, don't come unglued again. Yes, I promise."

"Turn your back."

"No way. I said I wouldn't touch, but you can't stop me from looking."

"Won't you spare me one iota of embarrassment?"

Gwen turned her back and began stripping away her wet clothes. When she was naked she asked with biting sarcasm, "May I have a towel now, Your Majesty?"

Chuckling, Zane got up from the bench, picked up two of the towels and brought them over to her. She cringed, but she let him drape one over her shoulders, then took the other from his hand and wrapped it around her waist.

It felt so good to be warm that she nearly swooned. But she showed not a drop of good cheer as she opened the sauna door and tossed out her wet clothes, to be worried about later.

For now, she would soak up the heat and listen to what Zane had to say. Although she couldn't imagine what topic could be so crucial that he'd go to this much trouble.

Fourteen

It was a large sauna, and except for where the heating equipment was situated the walls were lined with benches. Gwen sat on a different bench from the one Zane was using. Hugging the towels around herself, she tried not to even look at Zane as she said frostily, "Please say whatever's on your mind and get it over with. I can't hang around this—this den of iniquity the rest of the day."

He cocked an amused eyebrow and chuckled. "Den of iniquity?"

"Do you like the word *playpen* better?"

Zane turned onto his stomach so he could look at her. "Feeling a bit judgmental, are we?"

Gwen's ire rose again. "This isn't nearly as amusing as you seem to think it is, so stop your damn gloating. If there's anything I detest it's smugness—and an attitude of unwarranted superiority. The only area in which you're superior to me is your bank account."

"Really?"

"Yes, really. I don't know of one other adult who would behave as adolescently as you have today."

"Could it be that you have some very dull friends?"

"Could it be that *you* relate maturity with a boring existence? Should I take that as a sign that you haven't yet grown up?"

"Who pushed who into the pool?"

"Who threw the key in the pool?" she shouted. "And you didn't have to haul me in with you and then try to drown me!"

"Are you really mad, or do you just want me to think you are?"

Gwen's jaw dropped. "Are you totally crazy?"

Zane sat up. "Well, hell, what I did wasn't that bad. If you had the slightest idea of how to relax and have a little fun, you'd be laughing now instead of yelling at me."

"I suppose every other woman you nearly drowned in your pool came up laughing, which, of course, makes me a stick-in-the-mud. Well, sorry, sport, but I *still* don't think it's funny. And if you do, you have a very warped sense of humor."

"At least I have one," Zane said dryly.

Gwen glared at him. "Meaning that I don't?"

"I'm trying to remember if I've ever heard you laugh."

"Well, why don't you tax your brain for a *reason* for me to laugh!"

Zane thought about that for a moment, then sighed. "Okay, I know you've got it tough."

She had not been looking for sympathy, and embarrassment hit her so hard that she suddenly felt like bawling. Zane *knew* how she lived. He knew her financial situation and that she was the sole supporter of her children. He'd seen her house and her decrepit old van. He knew too much about her, way too much! How had she let that happen, when ordinarily she was so closemouthed about her problems? Ramona knew the truth of her life, of course, and so did Gwen's parents. But she had opened a door for Zane that was usually locked pretty tightly, and that wasn't like her at all.

Her voice wasn't quite steady when she spoke, but there were things that needed to be said. "I've made too many mistakes with you, Zane. Sleeping with you was probably the worst, but then again maybe taking that two thousand for deceiving your family was, all things considered, a lot worse than that. The thing is, everything that's happened between us was wrong, and it's almost impossible to pick out our worst sin. Maybe none of it was a sin or a crime for you, but it was for me. You see, you and I are very different people. We've been different since the day we were born, and our differences will only increase as we grow older."

She drew a breath. "I don't want your sympathy, Zane. I don't want *anyone's* sympathy. I might not have money, but what I do have is priceless."

"Your kids," Zane said softly.

"Yes, my kids."

Zane chewed on his lower lip. He should be telling Gwen about the incident with her father. In fact, he should have told her about it the moment she arrived, instead of luring her to the pool. But how did a man tell a woman something like that? He knew now, without the slightest doubt, that she wouldn't deem it funny and laugh about it. Her whole life was just too serious for her to find much humor in it.

He looked at her and felt guilty because he'd never had to experience what she did on a daily basis—financial insecurity in every possible shape and form. And he felt other things, too—a flood of affection and warmth and admiration for her spunk, and, of course, desire because she was a beautiful woman, in spite of the dunking she'd taken.

To heck with Jack Lafferty's weird ideas about his intentions, Zane thought then. Maybe he wasn't quite ready for marriage—and he should probably phone Jack and tell him that—but he and Gwen could still have something special going for them.

"I agree that mistakes were made since we met," he said quietly. "But they're not the ones you just mentioned." Rising, he moved from his bench to hers and sat next to her.

Gwen's eyes got big. "Zane, please don't make a pass."

He took her hand in his and gazed into her eyes. "Tell me again why you don't date."

"Be—because I don't have the, uh, time."

"Honey, we both know that's not true. Let me amend that. It's true to a point, but if a man was willing to see you on your timetable, then that excuse would vanish, wouldn't it?"

"You're not going to talk me into anything," she whispered, shaken by his nearness and the gleam of conviction in his eyes. She wished he would at least cover his lap; he was just too at ease with his nudity for her comfort.

"Gwen, all I want is to see you. San Antonio has some wonderful restaurants. Would having dinner with me once in a while be so terrible? Would simply talking to me on the phone take up too much of your time?"

"Why…why do you *want* to see me? Zane, don't you grasp how different we are from each other? Don't you understand what I tried to explain a minute ago?"

"Do you think I'd enjoy dating a clone of myself?

Gwen, your attitude doesn't make sense. You're a woman, I'm a man. Of course there are differences. Good Lord, it's the differences in people that make them interesting.''

"I was talking about...about social standing," she blurted, and then turned her head to avoid his eyes.

"Oh, I get it. You're not listed in the Texas social registry, so someone who *is* shouldn't like someone who isn't." Zane took her chin and turned her face toward him. "You're not really that kind of snob, are you?"

She had no immediate reply to what seemed a rather ludicrous question, and a silence lengthened until finally she said, "I'm simply not in your class, and you can call that snobbery if you wish, but that label is not going to change anything—certainly not how I feel about myself...or you."

"That's an opening, if I ever heard one. How *do* you feel about me? I'm talking about me now, Gwen—not my name, not my family, not my net worth, but me, only me."

She wilted. She was getting hot from the sauna, anyway, and being asked point-blank how she felt about him was too much to deal with.

He saw what he'd done to her and immediately became remorseful. He might not totally comprehend his feelings for Gwen, but he knew without doubt that he didn't want to discomfit her with difficult and maybe even unnecessary questions. Tenderly he put his arms around her and brought her head to his chest.

"You don't have to answer that," he whispered into her damp hair. "Let me tell you how I feel about you. You're a special human being, Gwen. I honestly have never met anyone like you before. You're a wonderful mother and a hard worker, and I've never heard you blame anyone else for your situation. On top of those great qualities, you're seriously beautiful and probably the most sensuous woman I've ever known. I'll say something else here. If you'd let me, I would give you the world. I hate your worrying about money, and—''

''Don't say it!'' She dropped her forehead to his bare chest with a muffled groan of utter humiliation. ''I would never take a penny from you or any other man. If you don't know that about me, you don't know anything.''

''I'm sorry, I do know that. Forgive me. I promise it will never happen again.'' He took her chin and tipped up her face, but this time he pressed his mouth to hers.

Tears welled in her eyes, but she was completely defeated and knew it. Maybe she'd known this was going to happen even before ringing his doorbell. She let him kiss her, and she parted her lips for his tongue. She kissed him back and let the towels around her fall away, then turned on the bench so that her bare breasts were against his chest.

''Oh, sweetheart,'' he moaned hoarsely, and settled them both on the bench so she was on her back and he was on top of her.

After a dozen feverish kisses to her mouth, her face, her breasts, she invited the final bliss by parting her legs. He wasted no time in complying, and in seconds she was gasping and writhing with him on that bench. They were both sweating, as much from the incredible passion of their lovemaking as from the temperature of the sauna.

I love you…love you…love you. Her mind repeated the words again and again, though she couldn't say them. It was the reason she hadn't been able to tell him how she felt about him when he'd asked. It was sad that she loved him so much, because even though he'd said some very nice things about his feelings for her, he hadn't even hinted at the word *love*.

But such was their relationship, and she knew now that she would find a way to make the time to see him for as long as he wanted. It would be a little like living on the edge of a precipice, always nervous and wondering when he would meet someone new and more exciting, but it seemed as though she no longer had a choice. Fate, or something, had decreed that she fall in love with Zane Fortune, and free will had nothing to do with it.

It was strange how that knowledge affected her. She wasn't going to fight him or his attentions anymore, and knowing that with such brilliant clarity seemed to destroy every sexual inhibition she'd ever possessed.

She wound her legs around his hips, drew him deeper inside and released a long, drawn-out sigh of supreme pleasure. "It's so good, Zane, so good. Don't stop...don't ever stop."

"Oh, baby," he whispered raggedly. "We fit together so perfectly I can't believe it. It's like we were created for each other."

"I know...I know." She pulled his head down for a voraciously hungry kiss, and their passions seemed to explode. In seconds they each went over the edge, and neither of them even tried to keep their powerful feelings quiet, as they'd done in her bed the first time they'd made love.

Zane roared and shouted her name, and Gwen panted and moaned until she was totally drained. She was still whimpering deep in her throat when Zane recovered enough of his normal strength to lift his head and look at her.

She looked back at him, straight into his beautiful blue eyes. "How can I fight this?" she said huskily.

"You can't. Neither can I. Why should we try?"

"We shouldn't."

"Meaning, you're not going to?" Amazement entered his eyes. Was she saying that she would see him, go out with him, continue to make love with him? Had he really accomplished that much this afternoon? Dare he even hope for so much?

"That's right," she whispered, and happiness suddenly bubbled within him. He smiled and brushed tendrils of hair back from her flushed face.

"You will never be sorry, I promise you," he said ardently, and kissed her mouth with such feeling that she felt tears fill her eyes.

"I'm not asking for promises," she whispered against his lips. "I'll never ask you for anything."

He heard the husky quality of her voice and again raised his head to see her face. The tears in her eyes shook him. "No one has a better right to expect promises from me," he said softly.

"Right now, that's probably true. Who knows what tomorrow will bring?" There was an underlying sadness in her voice, because with Zane she would be a fool to think that she was the final love of his life. While she knew in her soul that an affair with him was a fool's game, she wasn't irrational enough to bank on a future with him.

"Gwen…" A marriage proposal was lurking on the tip of Zane's tongue. It was, after all, what he'd told Jack he intended to do, and at this very special moment he could easily say the words.

Only, what Gwen had just said about tomorrow destroyed the impulse. Who knew better than he that he was as changeable as the wind? At this moment he loved Gwen madly, but he suspected the strong emotion was caused by the incredible sex they'd just shared. In fact, he was still inside her and he could feel himself becoming aroused again, which didn't happen often. He loved women and he loved sex, but it usually took more than a few minutes to recharge his batteries before he was ready for a second round.

Gwen felt what was happening to him and shook her head. "No, Zane, I can't. It's getting late and I have to pick up my kids."

He moved lazily within her, simply because he couldn't stop himself. "Will you see me later this evening?" he asked while pressing tender kisses to her forehead, her cheeks, her lips.

"If I can get Norma Blake to watch the kids, yes," she whispered as desire rose in her body again. "I'll call you when I get home and find out. Will you be here?"

"I wouldn't leave this house for any reason tonight. I'll be here to take your call, believe me." He gazed into her eyes for a long, poignant moment, then lightened up with a grin. "Come on, let's go take a shower. I'll put your wet clothes in the dryer. You should be ready to go in twenty minutes."

"Uh, there's something you should think about," Gwen said hesitantly. "I get pregnant very easily. We should always use protection."

"Yes, we should," Zane said slowly as he realized that she could be pregnant this very second. What if she was? How odd that he would be so remiss with

Gwen when he'd never been careless with any other
woman.

Pushing the unsettling subject to the back of his
mind, he got to his feet and held out his hand to help
Gwen up and off the bench.

It was during the drive from Kingston Estates to
Ramona's house that Gwen started feeling tense and
uneasy. What in heaven's name was she doing? Her
hands clenched around the steering wheel as her
stunned brain painted a vividly detailed picture of herself and Zane in his sauna. How could she have be-
haved so wantonly? What had happened to her since
meeting Zane Fortune? My Lord, was she even the
same woman who'd been happily married to a decent,
trustworthy man like Paul Hutton and given birth to
his three beautiful children?

And there was no glossing over what she'd done at
Zane's house, either. She had consented to having an
affair with him, she'd told him they must always use
protection, indicating an ongoing sexual liaison, and
she'd promised to see him tonight!

No, wait, she'd promised to see him *if* she could
find a baby-sitter.

It was a way out—for tonight, at least. She could
phone Zane and tell him that she had not been able to
get a sitter. It would give her some time to think this
through, she thought as her head began aching.

By the time she pulled into Ramona's driveway, her
head wasn't just aching, it was throbbing. She was also
feeling nauseated, which, strangely, gave her hope.
Maybe she'd caught a bug. Maybe her symptoms
weren't caused by guilt, self-disgust and remorse at
all, but by a fast-acting virus.

And then reality hit her. "Stop kidding yourself," she whispered shakily, and switched off the ignition. "The only virus you've come in contact with today is Zane Fortune!" She got out of the van and stumbled to Ramona's front door.

"Gwen! My goodness, you look awful. Are you ill?" Ramona exclaimed worriedly.

"It's just a headache, Ramona." The kids ran in and hugged her legs. Bending over, she kissed each of them. "Get your things," she told them, and off they went to obey.

"Can I get you something for that headache?" Ramona asked.

"Thanks, but I'll wait till I get home." To Gwen's chagrin, she started crying.

"Okay, that does it," Ramona said with a sympathetic but determined glint in her pretty, dark eyes. "Something's terribly wrong, and since I'm your best friend, you have to tell me."

Gwen tried to dry her eyes, but the tears just kept coming. "Oh, I don't want the kids seeing me this way."

"They won't." Ramona hurried out, and Gwen could hear her talking quietly to the children in the living room. She was back in the foyer in a minute. "They're going to watch a cartoon video while you and I talk. Come to the kitchen."

Blubbering, Gwen followed her friend and meekly swallowed the aspirin Ramona gave her, then sat at the table and waited for the water to boil for tea. Ramona put a box of tissues on the table, and Gwen blew her nose and wiped her eyes.

"Thanks. You really are a good friend."

"And right now you need one. How come? What happened to cause this?"

Gwen looked down at the wad of tissues in her hand. "I—I slept with—Zane," she finally whispered.

"Today?"

"Yes, I just came from his house."

Ramona looked troubled, but she made no comment until the tea was ready. Then she brought two cups to the table, placed one in front of Gwen and sat down with the other.

"Are you in love with him?" Ramona asked quietly.

"Yes."

"Is he in love with you?"

"No."

"Did you know those things before you slept with him?"

Gwen wiped away another tear attack. "Yes, I knew." She sniffled. "I haven't even told you the worst part." When Ramona said nothing, she continued. "I…led him to believe that I would have an affair with him. He thinks I'm going to get a sitter for tonight and—and go out with him. It…seemed perfectly logical while I was with him, but on the way here I— I started falling apart."

Ramona cleared her throat. "Was today the first time?"

"No," Gwen whispered so quietly that Ramona almost had to read her lips to decipher her answer. "It happened one other time—at my house. The night of the barbecue." She covered her face with her hands. "Oh, Ramona, what am I going to do?"

"How do you know he's not in love with you?"

Dropping her hands, Gwen glared at her. "Sorry I asked that. You just know, don't you?"

"He told me I'm a very special woman," Gwen said bitterly.

"Well, you are."

"Yes, I'm so special that millionaire bachelors are lined up at my door in droves. Ramona, a man like Zane Fortune wants only one thing from a woman like me, and I—I'm such a damn fool, I gave it to him."

"You're not a fool, and don't say that again. You're in love, and women in love sometimes do foolish things. Okay, you've faced that, and now you're wondering what you should do next. Gwen, you're the only person who can answer that question. I could give you all kinds of advice, but I'm not in your shoes, nor could I possibly feel for Zane what you do. Maybe if you talked to your mother—"

"God, no! Mom and Dad are already calling me fifteen times a day to ask if I have anything to tell them."

"Why on earth would they be doing that?"

Gwen sighed. "I'm not a hundred-percent sure, but I think it's because Donnie saw Zane on Saturday night and mentioned it when Mom was at my house the next day. She figured out that Zane had spent the night, and ever since I've been getting these weird phone calls from her and Dad."

"Okay, but why would they think you had something to tell them that they don't already know?"

"I have no idea."

"Well, knowing your folks as I do, I'm sure you'll find out what's going on in due course. Gwen, you're looking much better. Is your headache gone?"

"Just about. I'd better gather the brood and head

for home." Gwen got up. "Thanks for everything, especially for listening."

"You know I'm available anytime you need to talk.
And, Gwen, don't be too hard on yourself. Only another widow knows how lonely a woman can get
sleeping alone night after night."

Gwen put her arms around her friend for a hug.
"You're the best friend ever." She stepped back.
"See you tomorrow morning. Kids!" she called as she
left the kitchen. "It's time to go."

"You can't find a baby-sitter?" Zane said into the
phone. "What about that older lady I met at your
house the night we went to the movie?"

"She already had a job. Zane, I tried everyone I
know, but no one is available for tonight. I'm sorry,
but there's nothing I can do."

"There are professional baby-sitting services, you
know."

"No strangers, Zane. I draw the line at leaving my
kids with strangers."

"I could come to your house," he said softly, sug-
gestively.

"Yes, you could, but I would rather you didn't. If
you do decide to come over here, you should know
that you and I will do nothing more than sit in the
living room or kitchen. Do you get my drift?"

"Would you still keep us confined to the living
room or kitchen after they're sound asleep?"

"Absolutely. There'll be no more adult doings in
this house, Zane, not while I have young, impression-
able children."

"Well, hell," he muttered. "I'm really disappointed."

"I'm sure you are." Try as she might, Gwen could not keep her voice free of sarcasm.

"Sweetheart, you're not changing your mind about us, are you?"

"Maybe you shouldn't ask that question tonight."

"Gwen, what's wrong?"

She heard some panic in his voice and winced; it had not been her intention to upset him. She still hadn't made up her mind about whether or not to continue their relationship, and at the moment she was planning a quiet evening of soul-searching.

So she lied and said, as calmly as she could, "Nothing is wrong. I'll call you tomorrow."

"Call? I want to *see* you tomorrow! And why shouldn't I ask you that question tonight? Gwen, are you giving me the runaround?"

Her breath caught for a moment. The "runaround" was exactly what she was giving him. But she wasn't quite ready to tell the man she loved that she was not going to see him again, no matter how many headaches came of their relationship.

"I wouldn't do that," she said with a flirtatious coyness that took her completely by surprise. Apparently she could lay it on with the best of them, she realized. She just hadn't known that about herself because there'd been no reason to resort to such tactics before Zane.

He accepted her falsehood without question, simply because she'd spoken in a simpering female fashion, she thought. She nearly gagged over her own acting, but she swallowed the impulse and repeated sweetly, "I'll call you tomorrow."

This time he accepted that as well, and took out his lover's voice, it seemed, polished it a bit and said in a low and sexy manner, "I'll be waiting to hear from you."

"Good night, Zane."

"Good night, sweetheart."

She put down the phone, got up from her chair and went to take some more aspirin.

Her head was pounding unmercifully.

Fifteen

Gwen's evening of "soul-searching" was cut short when she fell asleep on the couch about an hour after tucking in the kids for the night. And the next day wasn't much better, as far as hitting on any brilliant answers. Gwen took care of her scheduled appointments, worried a lot about what would come out of her mouth when she talked to Zane—which she had to do at some point in the day—and avoided her house and answering machine to delay the inevitable. It depended on what she said to Zane, of course. Last night the old can't-find-a-baby-sitter excuse had worked, but what about later on today? Tonight?

The truth was that she had to make up her mind on a very basic level: Either she had to take Zane as he was and live with her decision without complaints, or get it across to him—using whatever means it took—that she was out of his life, and that was that.

Her love for the conceited jerk was the real problem, of course, and the biggest hurdle to any kind of sensible decision. Factions warred within her.

You will never be happy with an affair.

Maybe that's true, but will I be happy without Zane?

He doesn't love you.

Not now, but maybe in time?

Don't be a dunce!

Around noon Gwen pulled her van into the busy parking lot of a popular mall that contained a little take-out sandwich shop that she frequented about once a week. She went in, ordered her sandwich and a soft drink, and was walking back to her van when she heard someone calling her name.

"Gwen! Yoo-hoo, Gwen!"

Gwen stopped walking and looked around. Spotting an older woman whom she vaguely recognized as being a relative of some friend of her parents, she smiled. Thank goodness she remembered her name. "Hello, Helen."

Helen rushed up and hugged Gwen, sandwich bag and soft drink in one fell swoop. "I'm so *happy* for you, Gwen," the woman trilled.

Totally taken aback by so much enthusiasm for something Gwen couldn't begin to imagine, she smiled weakly. "Thanks…I think. Helen, I have no idea what you're talking about."

"Now, now, you mustn't be shy. Why, you've caught the most eligible bachelor in the entire county. You should be proud, young woman, proud. Your folks are, I know. They've been boasting to everyone, even strangers in restaurants, and I don't blame them a bit."

Gwen felt a sinking sensation in the pit of her stomach. "Boasting about what, Helen?"

"Your engagement to Zane Fortune, of course." Helen tittered. "Oh, my, you should see your face. I'll bet you thought Jack and Lillian were going to keep mum until the formal announcement, didn't you?"

Gwen could feel the color draining from her face. "Mom and Dad are telling people that Zane and I are..." Her voice failed her, and she finished in a shocked, near whisper. "...going to be married?"

"They're telling *everyone!* And why wouldn't they? Goodness," Helen gushed, "it's not every day that a woman lands a fish as big as Zane Fortune." Helen colored a little. "There I go, prattling on a bit too much. I'm sure you don't think of your fiancé as the biggest fish in the sea, but—"

"I'm sorry, I've got to go. Goodbye, Helen." Gwen walked away. Before she reached her van she came to a trash can, and she dropped her lunch into it.

Helen called, "But, Gwen, you didn't show me your ring!"

Saying nothing because she was actually afraid of what she *might* say, Gwen climbed into her van and drove from the parking lot. A few minutes later, weaving through traffic, she realized where she was heading—to her parents' house. Her dad might be home, he might not; but her mother probably was, and this couldn't wait. Twenty minutes later she drove into the Lafferty driveway and parked next to her father's pickup. He was here. *Good.* With a trembling hand, she turned off the ignition.

"How could they?" she whispered in a shaky little voice. "How could they do such a thing?"

Pulling herself together, she got out and walked around the house to the kitchen door, which she knew was only locked at night. Her parents were having lunch at the kitchen table, and they both saw her through the window in the door at the same time.

Grinning and chuckling all over the place, they jumped up and ran to greet her. She was hugged and kissed before she could stop them, then they stood back and looked like two cats who had just shared a canary.

Lillian spoke first. "It finally happened, didn't it? And you came to tell us in person. Honey, we are so happy for you. Aren't we, Jack?"

"He said he'd do the right thing, and by damn, he's a man of his word. You bet we're happy," Jack said and tried to hug his daughter again.

Only this time she eluded his embrace and held out her left hand. "Do you see a ring? What on earth made either of you think that Zane and I are engaged? My God, I almost passed out when Helen What's-her-face collared me in a parking lot and started gushing because I—as she put it—landed the biggest fish in the sea."

A confused look passed between Jack and Lillian. "Jack, you said—" Lillian began.

"I know what I said," he interrupted brusquely, then looked at his daughter. "Are you saying that Zane Fortune didn't propose to you?"

"Propose! Dad, what made you think Zane was going to propose? We have never talked about marriage, and I certainly do not anticipate any conversation on the subject in the near future, or…or anytime! This is crazy. Helen said you were boasting all over town about our engagement, even to strangers. My heavens, what if it gets back to Zane?"

"Listen, young woman," Jack said sternly. "I only told people what *I* heard straight from the horse's mouth. It was Zane himself who said he was going to propose."

Gwen's knees got wobbly. "When? When did he say that, and how did you happen to *hear* him say it?"

Jack suddenly didn't look quite so blustery. "Uh," he said it the day I went to his office."

"You went to his office?" Gwen all but fell onto a chair. This couldn't be happening, it couldn't be!

"Now, honey," Lillian said to her daughter after a worried glance at her husband. "I'm sure there's just some little misunderstanding. You shouldn't let yourself get so upset. Your father was only looking out for you and the kids, and Zane did tell him that he wanted to marry you."

"If you'd have him," Jack said gruffly. "That's what he said. 'I'll marry Gwen if she'll have me,' he said. Then he made me promise not to mention it to you until he had the chance to propose."

"When did you go to his office? What day?" Gwen demanded to know.

"Uh, it was about a week after you and the kids went to that big barbecue at the Fortune ranch. Shortly after Thanksgiving."

Gwen looked at her father with tears in her eyes. "What made you think that you had the right to do something so...so awful? I haven't been your little girl for a very long time, Dad. I know I haven't done everything right since Paul died, but neither you nor anyone else can say I haven't tried." Wiping her eyes, Gwen got to her feet. "If Zane really said what you told me he said, then it had to have been a result of coercion. Did you threaten him, Dad?"

"Uh…"

Jack looked to his wife for support, and Lillian said hastily, "Gwen, you're taking this all wrong."

"I'm taking it wrong? Well, let me explain something. I've seen Zane several times since the barbecue, and he had plenty of opportunity to propose. He has

never once even mentioned the word *marriage* to me.
Now, why don't *you* explain to me exactly how I
should be reacting to hearing from a woman I just
barely know that Zane and I are engaged? And then
to hearing that my father humiliated himself—and
me—by forcing Zane into committing to something he
has no intention of following through on?''

''If he doesn't, then he's a snake in the grass,'' Jack
declared heatedly. ''And he's using you, just like I
accused him of doing.''

''That's entirely possible,'' Gwen said wearily.
''Regardless, I pray the gossip never reaches Zane's
ears. But even worse would be if some of his family
got wind of it.''

''What would be so terrible about that?'' Jack said
sharply. ''There's some kind of scandal going on in
that family every darn day. Always has been, as far
back as I can remember. They should be thrilled and
thankful that a decent woman like you would even
want to marry into that family.''

''You don't know them, Dad, so you are not qual-
ified to judge them. I don't care how many scandals
you've heard about, they are nice people, and they've
been nice to me. I would be horribly embarrassed if
Zane's family heard about an engagement that never
has nor ever will take place.''

Gwen walked to the door. ''I'm going to go home.''
She looked imploringly at each parent. ''Please,
please, don't tell anyone else what Zane said under
duress.''

''But he did say it,'' Lillian said. ''Gwen, your father was not standing over him with a hammer, for
goodness sake. You're putting too much emphasis on

threats and duress. All Jack did was ask him his intentions.''

"Dad can be very intimidating," Gwen said quietly. "I'm sorry, Dad, but it's true.''

"Maybe he's a yellow coward," Jack muttered.

Gwen blinked. "He…never struck me as a coward," she said slowly.

"Well, how does *this* strike you? The building was crawling with security guards. He wouldn't have had to talk to me for two seconds if he hadn't wanted to. He wouldn't even have had to let me into his office!''

Gwen sucked in a startled breath. "Why *did* he let you into his office?''

Jack smiled smugly. "So he could tell me that he wanted to marry you, of course. Why else?''

Maria Cassidy wasn't feeling well, though she couldn't pinpoint any physical symptoms other than a throbbing, persistent headache. Lying on the bed in her motel room, she watched her son playing on the floor with a toy truck and tried very hard to remember something. It was something important that had to do with the boy, but she couldn't recall what it was.

Her son…her son. That was it! That adorable little boy *wasn't* her son. James had been kidnapped by… Maria's eyes narrowed to slits. James had been kidnapped by the Fortunes!

Her troubled gaze again rested on the small boy on the floor. Who was he? Her hands rose to cup her bursting head. If only the headache would go away, then her mind would clear. These attacks were becoming frequent and frightening; in her current state she couldn't remember when they had started. But once her mind cleared she would remember everything. Perhaps what frightened her most was that the memory lapses were falling closer together, and she feared that a time could come when she would recall nothing at all about herself.

Bits and pieces of memory merely alarmed her. Her life was somehow intertwined with the Fortune family. That was the one thing she never completely forgot.

Odd, she thought. The pain medication she'd taken earlier finally kicked in and she fell into a deep and dreamless sleep, leaving the child on the floor to fend for himself.

Zane walked the floor in his office—stopping at various windows to look out, frowning intently—and worried about Gwen. A knot in his gut felt like a dire prediction: Gwen was not going to see him again.

He tried to argue himself out of the feeling. She'd promised things would be different between them. But she'd also promised to see him last night and then phoned to say she couldn't find a baby-sitter.

It could have been true, but Zane kept wrangling with doubts and suspicions. And unquestionably some very unusual fears were taking him into uncharted waters. Even though Gwen had fought against a liaison, she had now become so much a part of his life that he couldn't visualize the future without her. He thought of her devotion to her children and her determination to support her little family with whatever work she could find, even going along with his idea to fool his family into thinking he was so involved with one particular woman that they would stop their infernal matchmaking.

Gwen had agreed to his idea because of her need for money, but had almost immediately regretted it because she had liked his family and felt that they liked her, as well. Zane regretted the prank too. Not his part in it, but the fact that he'd involved Gwen.

All in all, he was feeling pretty lousy and could only lay his discomfort on uncertainty. If Gwen *had* changed her mind about seeing him again, what could he do about it? Picturing himself on a lifelong quest to convince Gwen that she should let herself like—or even love—him was terribly demoralizing. And it wasn't at all like him, either. How had he let Gwen get so deeply under his skin?

The word *love* floated in and out of his brain. Was that his problem? Had he really and truly fallen in love?

The intercom between his office and Heather's desk beeped and her voice entered the room. "Zane, your sister Vanessa is on line eight. Will you take the call?"

Zane heaved a sigh. Vanessa was probably going to try once again to pin him down on that dinner date at her house for him and Gwen.

"I'll take it," he said, walked over to his desk and poked the button for line eight while he picked up the phone. "Hello, Vanessa," he said as he sank into his chair.

"Zane, you devil, how could you do this to me?"

There was a teasing note in Vanessa's voice, but it sounded rather forced, as though he had upset her in some way and she intended to use tact to let him know about it.

Having no idea what he might have done to unnerve his sister, he merely said, "Pardon?"

"Your engagement, silly. Your family shouldn't have to learn of it through the grapevine. Goodness, Zane—"

Stunned, Zane broke in. "My engagement?" His mouth went dry as he tried to make sense of this. Like every town and city in the country, San Antonio had a thriving grapevine, but how would something said by Jack Lafferty—he was the only one who could have started this rumor—reach Vanessa's ears?

"Your engagement to Gwen. Now I happen to think very highly of Gwen, but one or both of you should have let Dad and the rest of the family know how serious your relationship was becoming."

"Uh, how did you come by this news?"

"How did I come by it! Apparently I'm one of the last to hear that my brother is getting married, because the whole town is buzzing. Three of my friends called to talk about it, and the finale was receiving a call from that society columnist newspaper snoop, Maureen Hardeman. I told her that it was your business and that she should phone you if she wanted details. Hasn't she called you yet? Well, I'm sure she will. Zane, I simply do not understand why no one in the family knew anything about this until I called them."

"You talked to Dad?" Zane said weakly.

"And everyone else I could reach by phone. I finally decided to stop circling the issue and talk directly to you. When, exactly, did you and Gwen become engaged?"

Zane was thinking fast, or trying to. The whole city had him and Gwen engaged. Did Gwen know? Had she heard the gossip? He had to talk to Gwen about this before discussing it with anyone else, and that included his sister and even his father. Certainly he wasn't going to take any calls from Maureen Hardeman or any other reporter.

"Vanessa," he said quietly, "the reason I haven't talked to the family is that nothing's definite."

"Are you saying you're *not* engaged?" Vanessa sounded shocked and disappointed.

"I'm saying that nothing is definite," Zane repeated as firmly as he could manage, which came off pretty well considering his erratic pulse and internal upheaval. What had Lafferty done, bought a spot on the evening news to broadcast his daughter's engagement? Damn the man! He'd promised to keep quiet, but he'd obviously done some heavy-duty blabbing.

"Well, answer me this," Vanessa said sharply. "How does a rumor like this one get started if there's no truth to it?"

"Now you sound angry," Zane muttered, and then hastened to soothe his sister by adding, "Vanessa, you'll never stop gossip with anger. People have always loved to talk about the Fortunes, and they probably always will. You know that as well as I do."

"And that's all there is to it? Zane, are you telling me everything? You have been seeing quite a lot of Gwen, haven't you? And you did bring her to several family functions, you know. Zane, have you and Gwen talked about marriage? Maybe she told someone and that's how the rumor got started."

"No, neither of us has even mentioned the word," Zane said flatly. "And if we had, Gwen's not the type of woman to let the whole world into her personal life." *It didn't come from her. It came from her dad! Why didn't Jack keep his word?*

In the next instant Zane knew precisely why Jack hadn't kept his word. He was too thrilled and proud that his daughter had drawn the attention of a Fortune to keep it to himself—hardly an unforgivable offense.

And possibly, taking it one step further, Jack Lafferty would have been just as thrilled if his hardworking, spunky daughter had caught the attention of *any* decent guy. The Laffertys probably worried a great deal about their widowed daughter and their three little grandchildren.

"Listen, Vanessa," Zane said, "I have to run."

"All right," Vanessa said with a quiet sigh. "Thanks for taking my call."

After hanging up, Zane stared blankly out a window. If the city was "buzzing," as Vanessa had said, then the gossip would eventually reach Gwen's ears. Maybe it already had. Maybe it was the reason she'd called off their date last night. It would be an awful blow for a woman to hear that the town had her engaged to a man who had never even hinted at anything permanent between them.

"Damn!" Zane mumbled as he got to his feet. He grabbed his suit jacket and strode from his office to Heather's desk. Pulling on his jacket he said, "I'm leaving for the day. Please tell David Hancock to take over, and tell anyone else who might be looking for me that I can't be reached. Also, you might be getting some calls from reporters. Get rid of them. I'm not interested in interviews or anything else."

"You plan to be completely out of touch for the rest of the day?" Heather asked.

"Totally. I'll see you tomorrow."

Zane walked out.

Gwen was so on edge after leaving her parents' home that she drove straight to her own. Humiliation over her dad's going to Zane and asking his intentions tangled with curiosity over Jack's interpretation of the event. *So he could tell me that he wanted to marry you, of course. Why else?*

Why else, indeed? Why had Zane talked to her father in such a personal manner and then said nothing to her about it? For that matter, why hadn't Zane mentioned her father's visit? How dare the two of them discuss her and then not have the courtesy to tell her about the meeting? She was not a witless child, dammit!

Zane Big-Shot Fortune had no right at all to intrude on her little world and make her fall in love with him. Oh, yes, it was all his fault that she loved him, the rat. How could a woman like her *not* fall in love with a man like him? He should have left her alone.

Her head had started aching, and she knew the pain was caused by the tension in every cell of her body. Gwen fell onto the sofa and lay with one arm draped over her eyes. *Why did Zane tell Dad he was going to propose?*

She was still lying on the sofa, still angry, unhappy and disgusted, when her front doorbell rang. Slowly but with sudden anxiety, she lifted her arm from her eyes. It could be one or both of her parents at her door; it could be someone from the neighborhood who had seen her come home; or it could be a stranger—a salesperson perhaps. But something, an inner voice, told her it was Zane.

The anger she'd carried home with her brought her to her feet. She hadn't anticipated talking to Zane this soon, but maybe it was best. It had to be done, and she needed to be free of him and his persuasive ways. And, by heavens, this time she was not going to be influenced by his good looks or charm! This was it. The end. And the quicker he got the message, the better off she'd be.

Sixteen

Even though Gwen had known in her soul who was at her door, and even though she had approached the door with a nervous energy borne of anger and humiliation, when she actually saw Zane face-to-face and registered his remorseful, downcast expression, she experienced a strong sense of sympathy for him that came close to shattering her resolve.

"Gwen," he said sadly, taking in her pale complexion and the terrible disappointment in her eyes. "You know, don't you? Will you let me explain what happened?"

The sympathy faltered, and her mind became active again. She couldn't be soft about this. She'd been treated as a pawn, by Zane and her own father, and immediate forgiveness simply wasn't an option. She would have to get over it with her dad, just because he *was* her dad and had always been there for her. Things might be awkward between them for a while, but family bonds were not easily broken.

Zane, however, was a whole other ball game. They had no bond at all. Their one area of common ground was an insult to her sense of respectability. He'd barged into her little world without finesse or tact, and if she had encouraged him in any way it was because he was a daunting, overwhelming person and she'd had no experience whatsoever with a man of his nature and stature.

"I have only a few things to say to you," she said dully.

"All right, I agree that you deserve your day in court," Zane said slowly, "but may I come inside for the proceedings?"

Gwen didn't have to think about that request for long. She didn't trust Zane. And could she even trust herself when he'd proved again and again that she was definitely the weaker sex where he was concerned? She'd let things go much too far with Zane Fortune, and it was not going to happen again. Her heart was already broken; she didn't need it crushed into a million irreparable pieces.

"No, I don't think so," she told him.

"Gwen, we really do need to talk about this," he pleaded. "I should be entitled to present my side of it."

Her voice rose slightly. "Entitled? Do you actually have the gall to make reference to a person's rights? Were you thinking of *my* rights when...?" She shut her mouth tightly, though her eyes were practically shooting daggers at him.

"I don't intend to get into a debate with you," she said icily. "I don't want to ever see you again, and to ensure that, I'm giving you notice here and now that as of this moment your arrangement with Help-Mate is canceled."

Ignoring his stunned expression, she took a step back and started to shut the door, but then her gaze went beyond Zane to a blue minivan pulling up to the curb directly behind Zane's car. An attractively dressed woman got out; she smiled and waved, as though she were an old friend, then headed across Gwen's front lawn toward the house.

Gwen vaguely noticed that a young man also got out on the driver's side, but he merely walked around the minivan and stood there. He seemed to be holding a camera.

Zane turned to see what was going on behind him and groaned out loud, startling Gwen. By that time the woman had reached the small stoop, though she remained standing on the grass.

"Hello, Zane," the woman said with another big smile. "And this lovely lady has to be Gwen Hutton. Gwen, allow me to introduce myself. I'm Maureen Hardeman, and I'm a society news columnist with the *San Antonio Daily Star*."

"I...I've read your column for years," Gwen stammered, while wondering what on earth a well-known journalist was doing here.

"Have you really? How nice. I always enjoy meeting a fan."

Zane could tell that Gwen was mystified. But he wasn't. He'd had this tenacious reporter on his tail before, and he knew outright rudeness was really the only thing she understood.

"You're not getting an interview from either Gwen or me," he said brusquely. "So you might as well pack yourself back into that minivan and get moving."

Gwen gasped. "Zane!"

"Since Zane is throwing attitude around, I'll address my questions to you, Gwen," Maureen said, shooting Zane a dirty look, then smiling at Gwen.

"Questions?" Gwen echoed uneasily. "I don't understand."

Maureen pulled a notebook and pen from her large

shoulder bag. "Of course you do, dear. Have you and Mr. Fortune here set the date yet?"

Zane saw Gwen's skin go even paler than it had been. "Is *that* why you're here?" she asked weakly.

"It's exactly why she's here," Zane growled. "I'm not going to be a part of this, Gwen, so I'm leaving. You shouldn't be, either, but I guess that's up to you." He took the stairs to the lawn, then noticed the young man with the camera sneaking furtive shots of Gwen's house.

Gwen just happened to see the same thing at the same moment, and she didn't stop to think but instead rushed pell-mell down the few stairs, shouting, "Stop taking those pictures! How dare you intrude on my privacy?"

She tripped on something, tried desperately to regain her balance, got twisted up in her own feet and somehow ended up flat on her back, dazedly staring up at the sky. But she only saw cloudless blue for a moment. When Zane had seen her heading for a fall he rushed forward to save her, tripped himself and landed right on top of her.

"Get that shot!" Maureen yelled gleefully, and the *snap* and *whir* of the camera as the photographer took shot after shot seemed to deluge Gwen's brain. "Thanks, Zane," Maureen called cheerily as she and the young man climbed into the minivan and drove off laughing.

Zane looked into Gwen's eyes. "You're going to be in tomorrow's society section of the *Daily Star*," he told her. "We both are, and it's not going to be a flattering picture. Can you deal with it?"

"Do I have a choice?" Gwen pushed at him. "For crying out loud, get off me!" Freed from his weight, she got to her feet and brushed dry leaves and grass from her clothes. Then she turned on Zane. "You have brought me nothing but trouble from the day we met. I told you to leave me alone. I told you I don't date. Do you ever pay attention to anything anyone says? Don't bother to lie about it, I know you don't. You think you can do whatever strikes your fancy, never mind how someone else might feel about it."

He didn't like the deadly calmness of her voice. It gave a finality to her words that screeching at him never would have. He realized that he was losing her, right here on the front lawn of her home, before God and any neighbors that might be watching.

It was a completely unacceptable, devastating thought, and at that moment he knew he loved her, that he was *in* love with her. Madly, wildly in love. Gwen was the woman he wanted to spend the rest of his life with, and yes, her three kids were in that picture too. Not only that, he'd like to have children of his own.

Was this how it happened? he wondered in awe. One moment doubtful, the next so certain that a man felt thunderstruck?

He cleared his throat in preparation of telling Gwen his thoughts. There was no way, after all, that he could keep this from her. He didn't even take a few seconds to plan an opening, he just plunged right into it.

"I told your dad I wanted to marry you, if you would have me. I'm asking you now."

Gwen wondered if she'd hit her head when she'd tripped and fallen, and now she was imagining things.

"You're staring," Zane said softly. "Did I shock you? Scare you? Tell me what you're thinking."

She started crying. "You're always doing that.

Whenever I tell you to stay away from me, you come up with something that…that makes me sound silly. And foolish. And…and immature. And I'm not silly or immature. Or I wasn't until I met you. Now I don't know…what I am. Or even *who* I am. All I know is that I'm not the s-same person I used to be.''

He took her hands in his. ''That's because you're in love, and people in love behave strangely. I'm a perfect example. I didn't know my own mind until ten seconds ago, and now everything is so clear that I wonder what happened to the blinders that I had to have been wearing. Gwen, I love you. *I love you!*''

''No,'' she moaned. ''Don't say something you don't mean.'' She tried to pull her hands from his, but he hung on tightly.

''I *do* mean it. I love you and want to marry you. For God's sake, don't shoot me down when I'm flying so high. You have to love me back, you just have to.'' He ducked his head to be more on her level, and peered into her eyes. ''Go on, say it. And if you can't say it because it isn't true, then say *that*. But I have to know one way or the other. Sweetheart, do I stand a chance?''

Even though her eyes were still spilling tears, her throat and mouth were suddenly dry. Surely he wasn't serious. ''I…''

''Go on,'' he prompted. ''You what?''

With a desperate tug she managed to yank her hands free of his, and she started walking quickly toward her front door, which she'd left wide open.

Zane almost had to run to keep stride with her. ''I know why you're going in now,'' he said. ''So I'll follow and we can make love.''

She spun around so fast that she saw stars for a

second. "Do you get a kick out of taunting me? Tormenting me?"

"If you weren't in love with me, nothing I could do or say would torment you, Gwen. Damn, it's great to finally see the light. Now I know why some of the things you said and did drove me crazy. I was in love and didn't know it. And I would bet anything that you're having the same problem this very minute."

Throwing up her hands in a sign of absolute incredulity, Gwen continued on into the house. Zane was right behind her, of course. She hadn't even attempted to keep him from going in when she did.

After closing the door, she leaned against it, feeling weak and shaky and as though she were on an emotional roller coaster. "I...don't believe a word you said," she finally got out. "I think you would say anything to—to keep me in line. To keep *any* woman right where you want her until you're through with her."

"Even to propose marriage?" Zane let out a whoop of laughter. "Gwen, you obviously know nothing about my views on marriage."

"I know that you've done your damnedest to avoid it," she snapped. "The whole city knows it."

"Thanks to people like Maureen Hardeman, the entire population of this city *thinks* it knows all of the Fortunes," Zane snapped back. He gentled his tone. "But let's not digress. I *have* avoided marriage. More to the point, I've avoided marriage-minded women. But doesn't that very fact prompt an interesting question? Why didn't I avoid you, sweetheart? It's as obvious as the nose on your face that you're the marrying kind of woman, so why didn't I leave you be, as you asked me to? The answer is simple, so don't strain yourself.'' Zane grinned. ''Isn't it?''

''You're the most egotistical person I've ever met!''

''Quite possibly,'' Zane said agreeably.

''And you're spoiled rotten!''

Zane thought a moment. ''Probably.''

''And…and you think every woman you meet is— is fair game!''

''As a result of your first two observations, that one is quite likely. However, we are discussing the *old* Zane Fortune, not the man standing in front of you today with love in his heart and a marriage proposal on his lips.''

''Oh, please,'' she drawled, but try as she might she could not maintain the stern, forbidding expression she'd been holding since entering the house, and her lips twitched.

''Don't tell me!'' Zane cried dramatically. ''Could that be the start of a smile? Methinks it is possible.''

''Oh, for Pete's sake. What woman would want to marry such a hopelessly bad actor?''

''You?'' Zane held out his arms. ''Maybe?''

Tears sprang to her eyes as she stepped into his arms. ''Yes,'' she whispered. ''I'm a sucker for bad acting.''

''Say you love me. I am not going to kiss you until you say it.''

''I love you, you big jerk. I've loved you since the day we met.''

Zane chuckled, then sighed contentedly. ''Me too, sweetheart, me too.''

Gwen moved through the following days in a daze. As she said to Ramona, ''It doesn't feel real. Why

would a man who could have any woman in Texas
fall in love with me? I will probably never understand
that.''

She said something similar to her mother when
Zane drove her to the Laffertys to relate the good
news. Lillian was appalled at her daughter's low self-
esteem. ''My goodness, Gwen, your father and I are
so happy for you, and instead of counting your blessings you're looking for reasons why Zane shouldn't
love you. Well, when I look at you, I see the many
reasons why he does love you, and in my opinion he's
a very lucky man that you fell in love with *him*.''

Gwen's family and friends were ecstatic over her
engagement, and when Zane began taking her to *his*
family's homes to present his bride-to-be, no one gave
Gwen any cause to doubt that the Fortunes, too, were
thrilled with the liaison.

Regardless, when Gwen was alone she trembled
with uncertainty. Not because she didn't love Zane,
nor because she didn't believe in his love for her. It
was the idea of becoming a Fortune that shook her
very foundation. How did a woman who had squeezed
every cent out of every dollar she'd gotten her hands
on for most of her adult life make such a major tran-
sition?

The Fortunes' immense wealth was obvious in
every home Zane brought her to. Gwen truly felt like
the country mouse calling upon the city mouse. She
saw such splendor in the expensive clothes and jew-
elry her soon-to-be relatives wore so casually and
comfortably, and she tried to imagine herself gra-
ciously hostessing a dinner party in a fabulous dress,
and carrying it off with style and panache while making her guests feel completely at ease. It simply didn't

compute, and the awful thing was that although she knew' she should talk to Zane about her fears, she couldn't quite bring herself to do so.

Then came the dinner party in Zane's and her honor at Ryan Fortune's incredible mansion on the Double Crown Ranch. This was the event that Gwen had been dreading most. She had dined at Zane's sisters' and brothers' tables, been kissed and welcomed into the fold by cousins, aunts and uncles, but Ryan Fortune was the head of the family, and, to Gwen, a formidable figure, even though he'd spoken pleasantly to her on her previous visits to his ranch.

But the idea of talking to him as his future daughter-in-law scared the daylights out of Gwen. So did the dinner party itself, because she had nothing appropriate to wear to such an important occasion. She still hadn't accepted any money from Zane, though he'd tried to write her a check every time they saw each other. "Gwen, this is silly," he told her. "Things are different now. You're going to be my wife."

And so she swallowed her pride—which hurt like the devil—and let him write the check. When he handed it to her and she read the amount, she gasped, "Zane, this is for fifty thousand dollars! All I need is a new dress to wear to your father's dinner party!"

"You also need money for Christmas, and for a wedding dress, and how about old debts? Honey, I don't ever want you worrying about money again."

Gwen murmured a very quiet "Thank you," but deep in her soul she felt like a gold digger.

Nevertheless, she deposited the check into her account, paid off every debt she had except for her house mortgage—including what she owed her parents—and then went shopping. It was such fun buying Christmas gifts for her children, and for Ramona and her kids, and then for Zane and members of his family, and for her own parents, that she nearly forgot to look for a dress for herself.

Finally, though, she did look, and she found a little black number that appeared too severe on the hanger and then turned into a dream on her body. It was the perfect dress—she'd always liked black—and she spent the next two hours searching out the right accessories. It was an exhausting shopping trip, but she returned to her house pleased with her purchases, even if they had been bought with Zane's money.

It didn't surprise her that he was at her house when she got home. She'd given him a key, and he was waiting inside. He came outside when she drove into the driveway and helped her carry in her packages. "Did you buy a dress for Dad's party?" Zane asked.

"A fabulous dress. At least I think it is. Would you like me to try it on for you? I really would like your opinion."

"I'd love to see it. What's in all these other bags?"

"No peeking! Some of those packages are for you. While I change into my new dress, would you mind putting everything else in one of those empty cupboards in the garage? I'll sort and wrap when I have the time."

"Sure, no problem," Zane said amiably, but as she walked out of the room with her dress in a plastic bag and several other parcels in her hands, his thoughts changed direction. The children were still at Ramona's, he and Gwen were alone in the house, and just the sight of her had brought his body to life. He quietly walked down the hall to her bedroom—she hadn't shut the door—leaned against the woodwork and watched her undress.

Gwen was down to her bra and panties when she caught a glimpse of Zane in a mirror. From the expression on his face, he was a lot more interested in her than in her new dress. Her whole system went into meltdown, and since they hadn't made eye contact, she was pretty sure he wasn't aware that she'd spotted him in the mirror.

Oh, how she loved him! The wonder of so much love in her heart made her emotional, and she had to blink back tears. Turning around, she smiled tremulously. "You look like a man with something on his mind," she said softly.

"Yes," he said, and walked over to take her hands. "Gwen, I love you. Do you know that, do you feel it?"

"Yes," she whispered. "I know it. Can you tell how much I love *you?*"

He nodded. "I can tell. Sweetheart, I followed you to make love, but while I was watching you undress, a subject occurred to me that we haven't yet talked about."

"And that subject is?"

"Kids. Gwen, I love your three, and while I have no idea how I could be so positive, I know in my own soul that I'm going to be a good father to them. But…well, would you mind having at least one more child?"

She breathed a sigh of relief. He'd spoken so somberly that for a moment she'd become fearful. "Zane, I would be honored to have your baby. Oh, my darling, I would *love* for you and me to have a child."

He gathered her into his arms, but not so quickly

that she missed seeing the tears in his eyes. Her own misted over, and she snuggled close to her beloved. If they could remain as happy together as they were right now, she thought, they would have a wonderful marriage.

On the evening of Ryan's dinner party, Gwen brought her children over to Ramona's house just before Zane was scheduled to pick her up. The kids were excited because they were going to stay the night, and they rushed into Ramona's house with their little bags.

"Oh, Gwen, you look so beautiful," Ramona exclaimed, then smiled rather shyly. "I know you've got to go, but I have to tell you, I met someone. Actually, I've known him for years, because we attend the same church. But we never did more than say hello, and today he phoned and asked me out to dinner. His name is Frank Delaney, and he's very good-looking, and he lost his wife about the same time I became a widow. He has two kids too, same as me, and…" Ramona began winding down. "Anyway, I think something important is happening, and I wanted you to know."

Gwen gave her friend an emotional hug. "I'm so happy for you, Ramona. Oh, I wish I had the time to stay and hear every detail, but I'm sure Zane is already on his way to my house."

"We'll have plenty of time to talk about it. You go now and have a wonderful time."

Gwen mustered a smile that looked rather sickly. "You're the only person to whom I can admit that I'm scared spitless about tonight, Ramona. Promise you'll always be my friend."

"Of course I will."

Gwen kissed and hugged each of her children.

"Have fun but be sure to mind Ramona," she told them.

"We will," they chorused, then ran off giggling with Ramona's children.

After a quick goodbye to Ramona, Gwen hurried out to her van. It pleased her immensely that her best friend might finally have met a man who was worthy of her, and it was what occupied Gwen's thoughts as she drove home.

But once there, she started thinking of the evening ahead, worrying about it. Zane was waiting for her, and after a loving kiss and compliments about her outfit and how beautiful she looked, he told her they had better get going or they would be late arriving at the ranch. They got into his car and began the drive.

By the time they turned in to the ranch driveway, Gwen was feeling more relaxed. Zane had talked about his childhood, his brothers and sisters as children, and Gwen had found everything he'd said very interesting and sometimes funny.

It was when she saw at least a dozen cars parked around the mansion that she got tense again. "Zane," she murmured uneasily. "All these cars. I wonder who else was invited."

"I recognize a lot of these vehicles," Zane said. "Looks to me as though most of the family is here."

Gwen's pulse began racing nervously. "I thought it was just going to be your father and Lily tonight."

Zane started chuckling. "I bet I know what's happening. This is a surprise engagement party."

"Do you really think so?"

Zane switched off the ignition and turned to her. "Sweetheart, don't sound so frightened. Everyone in there already knows you, and you know them. It'll be fun.''

''Yes,'' Gwen said a bit hoarsely. ''I'm sure you're right.''

But even with Zane holding her arm, she approached Ryan's home with dread and a most peculiar but unshakable premonition: Something was going to go wrong tonight.

All she could do was pray that whatever it was wouldn't affect her and Zane's plans for a future together.

Seventeen

The Fortunes and their spouses crowded around the engaged couple the second they entered the house— eager, laughing and seemingly all talking at once. Gwen smiled at them and was pleased that she now knew most of their names. There was Dr. Lucinda Brightwater Fortune, married to Holden Fortune, one of Zane's cousins, and the Kincaids, Vanessa and Devin, and Sheriff Wyatt Grayhawk, engaged to Gabrielle, another cousin, and so on. Lily, as hostess, kissed Gwen's cheek and said with one of her beautiful smiles, "Welcome, my dear. You look especially lovely tonight."

Ryan stepped closer. "It's wonderful seeing you, Gwen. Don't let this noisy bunch throw you." Taking her hand he wound it around his arm, and the two of them led the parade to an elegant parlor. Gwen looked back and saw Zane walking and talking with his sister Vanessa.

The parlor was gorgeous and tastefully decorated for Christmas, with a fire in the large fireplace and soft music coming from concealed speakers. The room's furnishings, from the sofas to the smallest trinkets, were not only beautiful but inviting. As striking and luxurious as Ryan's mansion was, it looked lived in and comfortable.

Some of the family members sat down, but most

remained on their feet so they could move around and chat with others. Ryan, Lily and Gwen stood near the fireplace, and Gwen complimented Lily and Ryan on their Christmas decorations.

"Lily did it all," Ryan said with an adoring smile at his beloved fiancée.

Champagne in elegant crystal glasses was being served, and Gwen took one from the tray offered by a waiter. Zane, also with a glass of champagne, moved to stand next to her, a warm and loving smile on his face.

"Vanessa told me she planned this," he said in an undertone. "She decided we needed an engagement party, and with Christmas and Dad's wedding coming up and everyone so busy, our having dinner at the ranch tonight seemed to her like a good time to hold it."

Gwen murmured, "I admit that it took me by surprise, but I'm fine now." It was almost true. Certainly she was feeling more controlled than when they arrived.

"Well, surprise was apparently what they were aiming for." Zane smiled while letting his gaze sweep the room. He received a dozen smiles in return. Without question he and Gwen were the focus of tonight's affair, and it made him feel good that his family was so united in approval of his bride-to-be.

Ryan called for quiet, and the conversations stopped. "I'd like to propose a toast—"

Before Ryan could utter another word, the shrill voice of a woman—sounding as though it came from the front door of the house—caused everyone in the parlor to wonder out loud what in the world was going on.

Gwen saw Lily tense up and heard her whisper to Ryan, "That sounds like Maria."

"Maria's welcome here anytime, Lily." He patted Lily's hand. "Let me go and find out what the problem is, dearest." He started for the parlor entrance, then stopped and stared, as everyone else was doing.

Standing in the doorway was Maria, carrying a small child—a boy. The handsome youngster had dark blond hair and blue eyes, and while he was very still and quiet in Maria's arms, he didn't seem to be frightened by the many eyes appraising him.

Still, it wasn't just the presence of Maria and the child causing everyone to stare, it was the wild disarray of Maria's hair, the thick layer of red lipstick enlarging and distorting the shape of her lips and the haunted, glassy expression in her eyes.

A chill went up Gwen's spine. Something was terribly wrong. Maria had struck her as being very strange at their first meeting, but from her appearance this evening she had gone far beyond "strange." Gwen could tell that everyone else in the room felt the same way, because the silence was thick enough to slice. Everyone seemed to have frozen in place. Did no one know what to do next? Someone should do something, Gwen thought with growing concern.

She felt relief when she saw Lily begin to walk slowly toward her daughter. "Maria, we didn't expect to see you this evening. How are you, dear, and who is this handsome little fellow you have with you?"

Gwen frowned. No one had ever told her that Maria had a child, but wasn't the little boy her son? Maybe it wasn't Maria's wild-eyed appearance that had everyone staring—maybe it was the boy!

She felt Zane's hand close around hers, and the

physical connection gave her insight into the tension he was undergoing. It was what everyone in the room was feeling, Gwen suddenly realized. What was going on?

It took a minute, but Maria finally focused her crazed eyes on her mother. "I want James," she said loudly. "I came for James."

"And who is James, dear?" Lily asked quietly.

Maria's eyes darted to the faces watching her, and then stopped on Claudia and Matthew Fortune. "They have him," Maria spat.

A murmur went through the gathering, and Gwen heard Zane whisper, "Dad, she's talking about Taylor."

Claudia gasped out loud and would have rushed forward if her husband had not caught and held her back. "Not yet, darling," he whispered, and brought her head to his chest where she wept into his shirt and tie.

"And…and I want five million dollars," Maria said next. Her voice turned into a moan. "You owe me five million dollars." Her eyes suddenly turned hard and hateful. "Do you think I can live on nothing? Raise this—this kid on nothing?"

Gwen noticed Dr. Lucinda Brightwater Fortune sidling cautiously through her relatives toward Lily, Maria and the boy. Sheriff Wyatt Grayhawk and Devin Kincaid were also working their way closer to the trio.

"Of course you can't," Lily said in a soothing voice. "He's a beautiful child, Maria. You know I love children. May I hold him while Ryan gets you the money?"

"Yes," Ryan said, his expression congenial. "I'll go to my safe and get your money right away, Maria."

"I deserve it. I should have had it a long time ago," Maria said bitterly.

"Of course you should have," Lily said a soothing tone. "Please, Ryan, go and get the money."

"Go ahead and leave, Dad," Zane whispered. "Wyatt and Devin are going to have this under control very soon now."

"Keep an eye on Lily for me," Ryan whispered back. "It won't take me long to get what cash I have on hand from the safe."

"I will, don't worry," Zane assured him.

Gwen watched wide-eyed as the scene unfolded one anxious step at a time. Lucinda, Wyatt and Devin had gotten quite close, but Maria didn't seem to notice. She began mumbling incoherently, and Lily kept saying, "Everything's going to be all right now, Maria. You'll have all the money you need."

And then Lily asked again, "May I hold the boy?"

It seemed that Maria's mind became clearer, because she snapped, "When I get my money."

"Of course, dear," Lily quickly replied. "I understand."

Maria's garishly painted lips curled into a sneer. "You understand nothing, you never have, so stop lying to me and everyone else. You still think Ryan Fortune is going to marry you, and if you believe that, you would believe anything."

"Maria, he is going to marry me," Lily said quietly. "We're going to be married two days after Christmas. I sent you an invitation. You must have received it."

"Where did you send it?" Maria snarled. "You have no idea where I've been living, or *how* I've been living." Her arms were getting tired—the boy was becoming heavy—and she transferred him to her other hip.

Ryan walked in with a briefcase and set it on the carpet about four feet from Maria. "Here's your money, Maria."

"Let me see it!" She became so excited that she let the boy slide to the floor while she knelt down and opened the briefcase.

Lily quickly picked up the child as Claudia ran over to them. Wyatt and Devin made a dive for Maria and each grabbed one of her arms. Maria started screaming and tried to get loose, and Dr. Lucinda did her best to calm her down.

"It's Bryan, I know it is," Claudia cried as she took the boy from Lily. "My baby. Oh, my baby is back."

The room was in turmoil. Everyone was upset, moving around and talking loudly. Gwen clung to Zane's arm.

"Is that little boy Bryan? Was Maria the kidnapper? I don't understand all of this, Zane," she told him in a tremulous voice.

"I don't think anyone does," Zane said grimly. "Not yet, they don't."

Dr. Lucinda called Red Rock for an ambulance, then ran out to her car for her medical bag, returning with it to give Maria a tranquilizing injection. Wyatt and Devin held Maria down until the shot took effect. Then, when she was no longer shrieking and squirming hysterically, they put a pillow beneath her head and sat next to her on the carpet.

Claudia undressed the boy and began sobbing when she found the birthmark. "He is Bryan, he is."

The questions started in earnest, making the parlor buzz: How had Maria ended up with Bryan? Was she the kidnapper? Was Taylor really her child? And then, when they looked at poor Maria and the condition she was in, the questions died down and a great melancholy descended upon the group.

After an interval Maria began talking, more to herself than to anyone in the room. "Ryan will never marry Mother. She will never have any of their money. The Fortunes think they're so great, but I showed 'em. Going to that sperm bank, and getting impregnated with Matthew's sperm was a brilliant idea." Maria stopped to laugh, and it was definitely not the laugh of a sane person.

Lily began to weep, and Ryan gave her his handkerchief and put his arms around her. Maria rambled on. "And so James was born, Matthew's biological son, and no one knew." Maria's expression turned ugly. "But Matthew found out...or something... because now he has James and dared to change his name to Taylor.

"But I have Bryan...and I can't care for him any longer. I have no money, and it's Ryan Fortune's fault. He will never marry Mother."

Dr. Lucinda chanced a question. "Maria, how did you get Bryan?"

"It happened the day of his christening. I brought James to the nursery. I was going to present him to the Fortunes. Then demand the money and recognition that I deserved. I'd show Ryan for dumping my mother thirty years ago. But when I returned to get him he was gone—a ransom note in his place. Someone had taken him, thinking they had Bryan. I didn't know what to do so I took Bryan and moved the note to his crib. I knew no one would help get James back, but they would find him if they thought he was Bryan.''

The ambulance arrived, and Dr. Lucinda conferred with the paramedics, relating Maria's mental state. The medics strapped her to a gurney and put her in the ambulance. Lily and Ryan followed the ambulance to Red Rock in their own vehicles. Claudia and Matthew took Bryan to the hospital to be checked over.

Those who stayed behind hugged Gwen and Zane and said a solemn good-night. Finally everyone was gone except for Dallas, Zane's brother, and Maggie, Dallas's wife. They lived on the ranch in their own house, so they were in no rush to leave, and they felt bad that the engagement party had turned into something so traumatic. But even so, everyone was thrilled that Bryan had finally been returned.

"It's all right," Gwen told them. "I feel sorry for Lily, but everyone else must be so relieved."

"Lily is probably relieved too," Maggie said. "She's been worrying a great deal about Maria." Then she said, "Gwen, there's enough food in the kitchen to feed a small army. Let's you and me let the staff go home and set out supper for the four of us."

"Is that all right with you, Zane?" Gwen asked.

"Yes, of course," Zane replied.

Maggie led Gwen to the kitchen and told the staff that the party was over and they could leave. Some of them, the ones that knew Maggie well, asked about Maria and Bryan, and she answered their questions. Gwen saw the same incredulity and shock on their faces that she'd seen on the family members' faces.

When they were alone, she said quietly to Maggie, "No one ever suspected that Maria had Bryan?"

Maggie stopped with a handful of silverware. "A

while back—shortly before Hannah and Parker's wedding, I believe—Cole, Maria's brother, went to her trailer to see her, although she had never encouraged visitors. At any rate, she wasn't there. Cole peeked through a window and, I heard, saw some baby furniture. Since Maria had never mentioned even caring for someone else's child, let alone having her own baby, Cole became very suspicious and naturally thought of Bryan. I don't know how long he waited for Maria to come home, but when she didn't, he left.

"He went back later, but she wasn't there and neither were her things. She had learned about Cole's visit from a neighbor, and maybe was concerned that he'd seen too much. Now, of course, we know the reason she ran away, but at the time the only thing people could do was speculate. Cole thought he might be overreacting, so he never told Wyatt—the sheriff— about the incident. Since then no one has known where Maria was living. As I said before, Lily has been worried sick about her."

"Maggie, Maria was at Hannah and Parker's wedding. Didn't Cole think to ask her about what he'd seen?"

"I would think he would have," Maggie murmured. "To tell you the truth, Gwen, I haven't kept up on every detail of the investigation. Dallas and I have only been married a year, and I guess I've just been too busy being happy." Maggie frowned. "That sounds terribly selfish, doesn't it? And it's not a hundred-percent true, either. You see, my own family never had money, and I've had so many adjustments to make that—"

Gwen broke in excitedly. "Maggie, I'm going through exactly the same thing right now! Oh, please tell me how you did it. I've been driving myself crazy worrying about never really fitting in to the Fortune family, no matter how hard I try.''

"Gwen, you already fit in. So did I, even though I didn't know it. Not that your life won't change. As I said, I've had to make a lot of adjustments. But looking back, they were mostly adjustments in attitude. *My* attitude. Great wealth is so awe-inspiring to a woman who never had an extra dollar in her purse—and that was the way I lived before marrying Dallas.''

"Maggie, that's the way I live! It never occurred to me that someone else might have gone through the same agony because the man she fell in love with happened to be a Fortune.''

Maggie smiled. "It makes it a little easier to deal with, knowing that you aren't the only one, doesn't it?''

"It does, it really does. You and Dallas look so happy together.''

"We are. He's a wonderful man, Gwen, a wonderful husband and a great father.''

"You already have a baby?''

Maggie laughed. "I had a five-year-old son when we got married, and Dallas adopted him. You must have seen Travis the day of the barbecue.''

"I probably did. I'm sorry that I don't remember him.''

"Don't apologize. Everyone's kids were running all over the place, and you had your hands full with your own three and their two little friends.''

Gwen looked a bit sheepish. "Yes, well, I'm not proud of my motive for bringing Tommy and Liselle that day. I did it to shock Zane into the very real world of parenting. Until that day he hadn't even asked how many kids I had, even though I had told him I was a mother. I thought he simply wasn't interested in anything but…''

Gwen faltered and Maggie picked up the thread. ''But getting you into bed?'' she said with a grin.

''Don't tell me it was the same for you and Dallas!''

''Pretty darn close.'' She laughed. ''Gwen, let's get this food on the table. We can talk while we work.''

''Zane and Dallas are probably wondering what's taking us so long.'' Gwen could hardly believe how lighthearted she felt. Talking to Maggie had worked wonders.

While they set the table in a small dining room and carried in platters and bowls of food, they continued their conversation.

''Do you recall meeting my mother at Hannah's wedding?'' Maggie asked.

Gwen had to think a moment. Then her eyes widened. ''Rosita! Yes, of course I recall meeting her. And you know what she told me after looking at my palm, don't you?''

''Mama tells me just about everything,'' Maggie admitted. ''She was right, wasn't she? She usually is, you know. You and Zane are going to be married right after the first of the year, just as she predicted.''

''She also said we were going to have four children,'' Maggie said slowly. ''Do you think she was counting the three I already have?''

Maggie's dark eyes twinkled merrily. ''That's something she *didn't* tell me. Maybe you should ask Mama when you see her again.''

Ryan called while they were eating, and Zane and Dallas each got on an extension and spoke to their father. Maggie and Gwen waited at the table until their men returned.

Dallas spoke first. "The doctors checked Bryan over and the boy appears to be in good health. They would like him to stay the night for a few tests, but it's only a precautionary measure."

"Thank God," Maggie said quietly. "Claudia and Matthew must be in seventh heaven."

"I'm sure they are," Dallas replied.

Zane said, "Maria has officially confessed to the kidnapping, but her doctors are certain she will never go to prison. Her mental problems are severe and possibly irreversible. Whether or not that's true, she needs help badly. Dad said he was told that she will probably serve her sentence in a mental rehabilitation facility. For Lily's sake, I hope her condition is curable."

Dallas added, "Apparently Maria did a lot of talking during her confession. She said that everything she did was to protect her mother, whom she wholeheartedly believed was going to be taken advantage of by the Fortunes for a second time."

"A second time?" Maggie asked with a small frown. "When was the first time, or is that a figment of Maria's imagination?"

Dallas looked at his wife. "The first time was when our Uncle Cameron seduced Lily and she got pregnant with Cole."

"*What?*" Maggie gasped.

"Dad knew about it, but he didn't intend for the rest of us to ever know. Maria's rambling confession told just enough of the story that Dad figured we'd better hear the truth from him. What happened back then was that Dad and Lily were in love, but Uncle Cameron was spiteful and always tried to take what was Dad's—including Lily. He lied and told Lily that his and Dad's father, our grandfather, would never permit one of his sons to marry a woman who wasn't rich, and that Ryan had succumbed to pressure and was going to break off the affair.

"Lily was young and naive, and Cameron finally wore her down and seduced her. She knew right away that she'd made a horrible mistake, and she ran away from the ranch because she couldn't even look Dad in the eye anymore. Anyhow, she found out she was pregnant and talked to Cameron about it but all he offered her was an abortion.

"She chose to keep the baby and a longtime friend, Chester Cassidy, agreed to marry her and pass off the baby as his own. Lily and Chester had two more children together—Hannah and Maria. Years passed, Chester died, and Lily and Dad met again. You know the rest of the story."

"And Maria knew all of that?" Gwen asked.

"She figured out some of it because Cole has the Fortune birthmark," Zane said quietly. "Maria is...well, she's always been different, and I guess she couldn't help it. Mental illness is a terrible curse. When one is physically ill everyone rallies and sympathizes, but people rarely recognize mental illness in its early stages, and we tend to avoid those who behave erratically."

"Yes," Gwen said in a rueful whisper, recalling how she had practically run to get away from Maria on Hannah and Parker's wedding day. "It's all very sad," she added while wiping away a tear.

"Yes, it is," Maggie agreed, blinking back tears herself. "Dallas, this isn't going to come between your father and Lily, is it?"

"No," Dallas replied positively. "I don't think anything could come between them again." He rose. "Let's put away the rest of this food and call it a day. Zane, Gwen, I don't mean to be rude, but Maggie and I would like to go home, and I'm sure you two would like to do the same."

"Yes, it's time," Zane agreed.

They drove in silence for miles, each lost in their own thoughts. Then Gwen reached out a hand and laid it on Zane's arm.

"Are you all right, Zane?" she asked gently.

He took his left hand from the steering wheel and covered hers on his arm. "If you love me, then I'm all right," he said huskily.

"Please don't ever doubt it," she whispered emotionally.

He squeezed her hand, then returned his to the steering wheel. "Gwen, I was thinking of my family's history, and wondering if there's *anything* at least one Fortune hasn't experienced. Tonight was traumatic—no one could ever say it wasn't—but it brought Bryan back, and I know it made me count my blessings. I'd bet everyone who was there tonight feels the same."

"I know I do." Gwen took a tissue from her purse and dried her eyes. "I realized something quite profound tonight, Zane. I've known for a long time that I was in love with you, and it was an incredible moment when I finally believed that you loved me, as well. But tonight, for the first time, there's something in here—" she touched her chest "…that knows it's right. I never really thought it was, you know."

"Because I have money and you don't. Gwen—"

"No, wait, that's all over with, darling. You must

believe me.'' She was thinking of her little chat with Maggie in the kitchen, but it didn't seem right to talk about things that Maggie might have told her in confidence.

Then an impish impulse struck her. They needed something to laugh about. Tonight's events had been so deathly serious, and it would be good if they could lighten up a little.

"Actually, dahling," she said with an exaggerated drawl, "I'm looking forward to spending your money."

Zane's head jerked around from downright shock, then he caught on and let out a whoop of laughter.

"Yes, dahling," he returned in kind. "How about the two of us spending my money together?"

"That sounds divine, dahling, simply divine."

The rest of the trip back to San Antonio was filled with jokes, laughter and very bad accents. But it was lighthearted, and lighter hearts were what they both needed that night.

Christmas was a wondrous day for Gwen. Santa had been especially generous with her children. Zane came over in the morning and stayed all day. Her parents, Ramona and her kids came for dinner, all with more gifts. By the time Gwen closed her eyes late that night, she felt as though she were floating on a heavenly cloud of complete and utter bliss.

Two days later she got dressed in a fabulous new outfit and went with Zane to Ryan and Lily's wedding.

How different this arrival was from her arrival at the first wedding she'd attended at the Double Crown Ranch! Now she was on Zane's arm as his intended bride, and she felt like a part of the Fortune family, even if it wouldn't be official until the fifth of January, the date they had set for their own wedding.

The house and grounds were decorated so beautifully—Hannah's work, obviously—that Gwen got teary-eyed. Everyone was there—all of Ryan's and Lily's children and friends, except for poor Maria, of course. And it was indeed a joyful if emotional affair. The ceremony made a lot of people cry. Maria *should* have been there. How sad it was that instead she was incarcerated in a mental institution, Gwen thought, knowing in her heart that the tear she saw in the corner of Lily's eye was for Maria on this happiest of days for herself.

After the ceremony the reception began, and dozens of people offered toasts to the newlyweds.

Ryan could not have been happier. His and Lily's wedding was the biggest, most lavish Texas-style wedding in recent history, and they were surrounded by loving friends and family. Even some distant relatives had attended, coming from far and wide. Ryan scanned the crowd. There was Cole, Lily's son, and his bride-to-be, Annie Jones, and Lily's daughter Hannah with her husband, Parker Malone.

All of Ryan's children were present: Matthew, Zane, Dallas, Vanessa and Victoria. Matthew and Claudia were now the proud parents of two beautiful boys, Bryan and Taylor. Vanessa and Devin were expecting Ryan's next grandchild, and Dallas and Maggie were also expecting a second child.

Holden and Logan, Ryan's nephews, had brought their new brides to their uncle's wedding, and others caught Ryan's eye: Jace Lockhart and his new wife, actress and screenplay writer, Ciara Wilde, and Ryan's long lost sister Miranda Fortune, who had come to the

Double Crown Ranch in anticipation of her daughter Gabrielle's wedding to Wyatt Grayhawk.

Ryan lifted his glass of champagne to another toast, then heard Sam Waterman's voice. Sam had been hired shortly after Bryan's disappearance to help with the investigation, but there was no question that he'd become a friend. But Sam wasn't merely making a toast to the newlyweds.

"Ryan, Lily, I'm sure you'll pardon my taking this opportunity to make an announcement. Mary Ellen and I eloped and were married at a civil ceremony in Austin."

Mary Ellen was the widow of Ryan's deceased brother, Cameron. Her marriage to Sam, a man that Ryan respected and liked, felt like a special gift to Ryan on his own wedding day. He squeezed Lily's hand and offered a toast to Sam and Mary Ellen. The event progressed joyously.

Zane held up his glass of champagne to Gwen. "Soon it will be our day, my love," he said softly. "Did I tell you how beautiful you look today?"

"A dozen times, my darling," she whispered.

A devilish gleam entered his blue eyes. "Did I ever show you the bedroom I used in this house until I went away to college?"

"No," she said quite calmly, belying the quickening beat of her heart. "You never did."

"Your education could never be considered complete unless you saw that room."

"I'm sure you're right."

Zane finished off his champagne in one gulp, then took her drink from her hand and set both glasses on a nearby table. "Come on, sweetheart, there's something in that room you have to see." He chuckled. "Or there will be when we get there."

"You are a wicked, wicked man." But she let him take her hand and lead her through the crowd.

They were almost out of room when a man who bore a striking resemblance to Ryan said, "My name is Teddy Fortune. I saw a news report about your family—about the kidnapping of Bryan and the parallel of that case to the kidnapping of Kingston Fortune's first son in 1942. I know this might sound crazy, but I think I'm related to you."

Zane stopped and turned to look at the man. "Well, I'll be damned," Zane said under his breath.

"Who is he?" Gwen asked anxiously.

"That, my love, is a whole other story," Zane said with an astonished shake of his head. "A whole other story."

*   *   *   *   *

*Over the next five months, watch
as more Fortunes find love and passion
in the Silhouette Desire miniseries,*

FORTUNE'S CHILDREN: THE GROOMS.

*BRIDE OF FORTUNE
by Leanne Banks
Coming September 2000
only from Silhouette Desire*

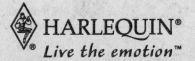

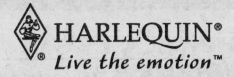

HARLEQUIN®
Live the emotion™

Upbeat,
All-American Romances

flip**side**

Romantic Comedy

 Harlequin Historicals®

Historical,
Romantic Adventure

HARLEQUIN®
INTRIGUE

Romantic Suspense

HARLEQUIN®
HARLEQUIN ROMANCE®

The essence of
modern romance

HARLEQUIN®
Presents

Seduction and passion
guaranteed

HARLEQUIN® Super**ROMANCE**®

Emotional,
Exciting, Unexpected

Temptation

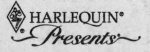

Sassy, Sexy, Seductive!

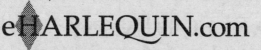

From first love to forever, these love stories
are fairy tale romances for today's woman.

Modern, passionate reads that are powerful and provocative.

Emotional, compelling stories that capture the intensity
of living, loving and creating a family in today's world.

A roller-coaster read that delivers romantic thrills
in a world of suspense, adventure and more.